CURSED AT BIRTH

CURSED AT BIRTH

Book One

STEPHEN NNAMDI

iUniverse, Inc.
Bloomington

Cursed at Birth
Book One

iUniverse books may be ordered through booksellers or by contacting:

iUniverse
1663 Liberty Drive
Bloomington, IN 47403
www.iuniverse.com
1-800-Authors (1-800-288-4677)

ISBN: 978-1-4759-8119-3 (sc)
ISBN: 978-1-4759-8118-6 (hc)
ISBN: 978-1-4759-8117-9 (ebk)

Library of Congress Control Number: 2013906350

Printed in the United States of America

iUniverse rev. date: 04/04/2013

Contents

1

THE CALL

Mannie groans, and I hit the morphine drip for him again. The poor bastard looked like a blackened steak when I hauled his skinny ass out of the inferno after the welding torch he was working with at the factory inexplicably flamed out of control and set him on fire about two weeks ago. Now, though, he looks more like a five-foot-ten-inch rotund petrified mummy. His entire head is all wrapped up in bandages, except for his eyes, nose, and mouth. I mean, man, even the guy's curly black nose hair is gone, and that's freakin' gnarly, I can tell you that!

As I sit with my coworker in the burn unit, I can still smell that awful sickly-sweet odor of charbroiled flesh. I doubt I'll ever be able to eat another steak dinner again. Even now, I feel as if I'm going to puke just thinking about seeing the guy going up in flames. And, sure enough, up the bile comes, all rumble-tumble-gurgle, and I force myself to swallow it back down. I take a big swig from the bottle of Penguin Ice I bought for a buck and a half at the vending machine down the hall, and the cool water soothes my throat, makes me feel alive, whereas poor Mannie probably doesn't give a damn if he dies. Probably he wants to die, at least that's what I think, but you never know.

He had been trying to tell me something just before it happened, something funky about work, and I'd listened only about halfway. You know how it is. A dude tells you something you don't care about and you just nod and say "uh-huh," and then you forget whatever the hell was just said. In one ear, out the other. Nobody listens anymore. I'm no exception. But as I think about how weird it was when Mannie started to burn and how weird it was that he became a human Roman candle right after he said that our boss, Paul Brouchard, was the devil, I get a cold feeling all over. It's as if I'm stepping onto a glacier for a sec. I don't like the feeling.

"Hey, Mannie, you awake?" I ask. *He ain't talkin' yet,* I think. *The dude's out cold, man!* "Come on, dude," I say. "Wake your sorry ass up!"

I pause, take another sip of Penguin, and decide I should bag it and go home to grab some dinner and some shut-eye before work. It's been spooky working security on the night shift since Mannie's accident. Everyone is on edge—and rightfully so. Everybody's wondering who's gonna be next. That's enough to give even a moron a bit of the heebie-jeebies. Sue Young, the drop-dead chick from HR, told us all to take it easy. She knows everybody's wound up tight.

"Y'all just chill out now," she said at the company meeting held just after Mannie went flame-o. "What happened to Mannie is just terrible, but we got to keep a stiff upper lip!"

Sue is from South Carolina, of all places, and I can't for the life of me figure out what she's doing in Canada, but there you go! She's here, even though she bitches about not being able to get grits and biscuits with gravy with her egg orders for breakfast. She bitches about a lot of things, but we all put up with her, mostly because she's a real sweetheart. The fact that she's cute as a button doesn't hurt either.

"This Canadian bacon, I mean, honey, what the heck is that all about?" she's been known to say. "Gimme some real pork any day!"

I have Sue to thank for the call that brought me into the big, bad world of Paul Brouchard and his creepy metal-parts fabrication factory. She called the security agency that hires me out as a long-term temp rent-a-cop, all in a panic, after the guard who was supposed to show up took a flyer. I came in for my interview, sat down in the hard-back chair in front of her messy desk, and gazed into her baby-blue eyes.

"Welcome, Mr. Abraham," she said, shaking my hand. Her skin was cool and soft.

"Michael. Please call me Michael," I said.

She smiled some more. "Okay, then. Michael it is! Tell me a little bit about yourself."

We chatted, and then she introduced me to the boss man. He gave me a firm handshake and a big smile, and then he dismissed me as if I were an empty pizza box. Once we were back in Sue's office, we sat down again. "I think you're gonna work out just fine," she said. "Can you start tonight?"

I said sure, and that was it. Since I work the graveyard shift, I almost never see Paul Brouchard, and I sadly don't see much of Sue either. You might say it was a bait and switch, but I'm not really complaining all that much about it. I do see halls, offices, bathrooms, the loading dock, the parking lot with its orange security lights, the rows upon rows of boxes and big metal parts in the warehouse, the busy factory floor bathed in bright fluorescent lights, and even the stinky restrooms while I make my rounds. Then I kick back and watch late-night TV in the guard shack. Workers tap and bang and torch and assemble the metal components used for any number of applications I don't know or care about. A job is a job, I suppose, even though this one is about as boring as it gets. It could be worse, I guess. I could be Mannie!

"Dude, wake up, man!" I say.

Mannie groans again. This time I don't hit the morphine drip. I poke him gently in the ribs, one place the flames didn't barbecue.

"Wha-what the—"

"Mannie! It's me! Michael!" I say, hunching low enough to speak softly into his ear.

"Michael?" he asks.

"Yeah, man. Michael."

"Oh."

"You gonna be okay, man," I say, and I wonder if Mannie can tell that I'm lying through my teeth. He's not gonna be okay. The man's toast, but there's no sense in saying so. I think he's figured that out already.

"You're full of bullshit," Mannie says, confirming my thoughts.

I laugh. "You're not supposed to cuss me out, remember? Paul's orders. Boss's orders. Cussin' offends his preacherly proclivities."

"Screw him," Mannie says. "He's the devil."

Mannie has been going on about that for days. I hate the job, and I hate the night supervisor, a blowhard named Jean Claude, even worse. That man never gives me a break. He's always busting my balls. Now, if Mannie had said J. C., the dickwad, was the devil, I might have believed it, but Paul Brouchard? Doesn't seem possible. He's a pretty mild-mannered sort of dude. He's roughly my height, say just north of six feet. He's got perfect white teeth and bright green eyes that set off his jet-black hair. Not sure what race he's running with, but he's definitely not solely European in ancestry. He seems smart, and he's very soft-spoken. He's also something of a recluse, or so I'm told around the water cooler.

"He's not the devil, man," I say. "That's just the good dope they're pumping into you, that's all. You gonna be right as rain. You'll see. Forget about this devil crap, and just get better. The night shift ain't the same without your sorry ass to razz."

"Y-y-you don't understand," he says quietly. His voice is so low I have to lean over real close just to hear him.

"I seen the guy, man," Mannie whispers. "I seen him turn into this creature thing—like, uh, some *real nasty* creature thing, man! With horns and a tail. The whole enchilada!"

"Sure, Mannie."

"No, man! I'm serious! A while back, near the night supervisor's office, the door is open a crack, and I see this weird red candle flickering. I hear this kind of chanting or something, and it creeps me out! I'm about to turn away when I see this shadow thing go, like—uh, well, take shape right there! It's the devil creature, and it gives me a real mean-ass look."

"Uh-huh," I say, not really believing him. The fire I rescued Mannie from is way too strange as it is. I think my friend's gone off the deep end with this devil talk. And yet that creepy feeling comes over me again, and I can't quite shake it. "You were probably smokin' too much BC bud, Mannie," I say. "Hey, man! That's probably why you got toasted. Burnt in the head while working that torch!"

4

"I'm tellin' you, Michael, there's some funky kind of stuff going on at work!"

I remain silent for a long moment, and then I say, "But seriously. You feeling any better?"

"What you think?"

I say nothing. Mannie coughs. He makes a moaning sound.

"I feel like crap," he whispers.

"I think I better go," I say. "I just wanted to see how you were."

"Thanks, man," Mannie says. "Thanks. I know you don't believe me about what I saw. That's cool, I guess. You just watch your ass, man, okay?"

"Sure, Mannie," I say.

As I stand up to go, the entire room goes cold. Ice cold. I sense something behind me, a presence, an evil presence, and I whirl around, hoping to surprise whatever it is. Out of the corner of my eye I see something.

"What the—?" I say. And in a sec the shadow disappears.

"Don't let it get me!" Mannie screams. "Don't—"

2

THE VISITOR

The present, Montreal, hospital burn unit, Monday, 4:15 p.m.

I freeze. My eyes bug out as I scan the room again. I sense that whatever it is hasn't left yet. It's hiding is all, and I feel its eyes on me even though I can't see a damn thing but what's supposed to be there—the bed and machines and the sunlit window framed in blue sky. Mannie's mouth is wide open, but nothing's coming out of it except a weird kind of slurping noise.

"Mannie! You see that?" I ask.

Mannie closes his mouth and nods just a little. Guess it must hurt like hell to nod, in his condition.

"I think it's still here," I whisper.

Suddenly, a shadow forms right in front of me. It's black, like a black hole in space. I can't see through it. It doesn't look like anything. Just a big nasty black blob that's pulsing, expanding, and contracting. It's about the size of a dwarf, and it's just floating there.

"Ma-Man-Mannie!" I hiss. "Dude, man! What the hell?"

The shadow moves closer to me. I back up. It moves closer. I back up again. It's toying with me, and I start to get pissed.

"You want a piece of me?" I say, forcing my voice to sound tough. As if I'm gonna kick ass on the blob. "Well, bring it on, bad boy!"

I move closer to the shadow. The shadow backs up. I move closer still. This time the shadow doesn't move at all. Instead, it starts to take shape. It gets bigger, and suddenly it sprouts two skinny legs with knobby knees, and flipper feet with toenails that needed a trim about a thousand years ago. Then I see it grow a tail.

"Oh, man!"

Mannie opens his mouth again. "Don't, don't let it, *don't let it get me!*"

"I got you covered, bro!" I say, but in reality I'm about to pee my pants. My asshole puckers and I feel as if I got water in my knees.

The shadow takes the shape of a man with horns and bright-red eyes. I half expect it to have a pitchfork, but it doesn't. I step back. It stays where it is. I'm wondering what will happen next, when the shadow's face morphs into the face of Paul Brouchard. I swear to God, the creature looks like my freakin' boss! I want to punch it in the nose, except it doesn't have one. I raise my fist anyway and shout, "You keep back! Stay back, devil face!"

The creature grins, revealing a set of choppers Jaws would envy.

"Oh no!" I shout.

"Oh, help!" Mannie screams.

"Oh, fuck, man!" I yell.

In a fit of desperation, I run straight at the creature. It vanishes into thin air. Just like that—it's gone! *Poof!* I wonder whether I even saw the thing, or if it was some kind of delayed shock from before, from when I hauled Mannie out of the flames. Mannie groans. I take several deep breaths, but I'm still hyperventilating. My heart is pounding as though I've just run a marathon in my black leather pants and tight black muscle shirt. Feeling a little calmer, I say, "Is that the same thing you've been seeing at work?"

"Yeah, man! That was it," Mannie says, his voice shaky and thin. "That's Brouchard. Dude set me on fire, man! On fire!"

I don't quite know what to make of that. I say, "Well, man, whatever it was, it's gone now."

"It's gonna come back, Michael," Mannie says. "It's gonna come back and get me real good. You'll see. I'm devil bait, man!"

I think on that for a few seconds. I hate to admit it, but Mannie might just be right. If that thing wants his ass, it's probably going to get it without any real trouble at all. "No, you're not, dude!" I say, lying again and feeling a little bad about it. "I'll get you a cross or something. Some garlic, maybe?"

Mannie groans.

"A silver bullet? A stake of hol—"

"Shut up, man!"

"Hey!"

"Go away, dickhead," he says. "Just leave me alone."

"Hey, man, I'm sorry! Okay?"

"Yeah. Right."

I say a few more words to my friend, and then I leave. I don't sense the creature anymore, but I'm worried about Mannie as I ride the elevator down to the main concourse of the hospital, fighting the pangs of claustrophobia I always get in enclosed spaces. I stride through the automatic glass doors in front of the building and put on my shades to cut the glare of the bright August sun. The weather is balmy, somewhere in the low eighties, a gorgeous day in my favorite city in the world. My parents came to Canada from Israel, but I was born in California when my dad was down there on business, so I am a dual citizen. They loved their native land, but they decided to leave just the same, hoping to escape the mounting tensions in the Middle East and give me a life of peace and security.

As a dual citizen of the United States and Canada, I have my feet in two distinctly cool places on the planet, and that's the way I like it. I speak English with a French accent from my time in Quebec, where I learned to speak fluent French, and I still use a lot of the surfer lingo from my time in Southern California, where the babes were hot. Smokin' hot! I'm also a practicing Jew, though I'm not overly zealous about it. My dad made sure I knew the teachings of the Torah, the difference between right and wrong, and what Yahweh wanted from me in terms of living a life of purity. I'm not so sure I've held up my end on that score, but when times really get tough I find great comfort in my religion. I think that's a good thing.

For example, the loss of my mother to colon cancer at an early age left me adrift emotionally. And even with Yahweh's help I never did get over her death, not all the way, anyway. Can a person ever fully heal when a loved one is ripped away like that? I don't think so. The scars are always there, even though the wound is closed. But because of my strong religious beliefs, I think I was better able to cope with my mother's tragic death.

In spite of my deep religious convictions, I have fallen down on the job, so to speak. I suppose my mother's death and the fact that my dad was a bit distant after Mom died contributed to my wandering tendencies, my inability to settle down, get married, and have kids of my own. I've drifted from one dead-end job to the next, and now that I'm just south of thirty, it seems too late to turn things around, even though I'm still pretty young when you look at the big picture of things. In dark moments, I turn to Yahweh, and I just keep on truckin', as the Grateful Dead say, continuing the long, strange trip.

This crap with Mannie and that freaky creature have made things way strange right now. Way strange! And I'm not sure how I feel about that. Part of me wants to cut and run, the way I always do. But part of me wants to find out just what the hell is going on with Paul Brouchard and his factory.

I find my old Toyota—kind of a pussy car for me, but reliable—and get into the front seat. I switch on the radio and let the hip-hop rip. I light a cigarette, take a big drag, and lean my head back on the headrest, blowing puffs of gray smoke out the window and wishing I could still smoke dope. Random drug testing put a stop to that habit, but I still get cravings every now and then, like now. I close my eyes and keep seeing that black shadow morphing into that creature. I tell myself I was seeing things, but deep down I don't believe it. Mannie saw it too. We both saw it.

What the hell was that? I wonder. *What exactly did I see?*

I'm suddenly very tired. Bone tired. I need some food and rest. I turn the key in the ignition. The engine fires up. I pull into traffic, the baseline of the song vibrating the car when I stop at the light. I turn left and head back to my apartment across the city, in the cheap section, and I try to forget about everything. The only problem is that I can't forget. Those bright-red eyes, the long, slender reptilian tail, the shark teeth, the way that the shadow blotted everything out into an impenetrable blackness—it all swirls and whirls around in my mind's eye as I drive like a zombie toward my seedy apartment. There I eat some leftover Chinese food, set the alarm, and get into bed.

Everything fades into oblivion—until I wake up screaming.

3

THE CURSE

Puncak Highlands, south of Jakarta, Indonesia, 1969

Shiheid Sabbah relaxed in his small ramshackle home nestled among the forested hills south of the teeming city of Jakarta, the jewel that sparkled and lured rich tourists to flock to the Java Sea for the sunshine and beaches. Inland, far from the wealth and the surrounding slums of the city, holy men like Sabbah were able to make lives for themselves and for their families through teaching the wisdom of Allah to the many. It was always rewarding for Sabbah when he conveyed his wise counsel to the confused or spiritually lost villagers who revered him, though he secretly did not believe in Allah at all. He believed in an entity Allah would condemn.

As a nonbeliever disguised as a teacher, Sabbah took a perverse delight in his manipulation of the people. They followed him blindly, never suspecting what he really was. It always gave him a sense of power in the way of things in the world at large when he was in control—because of his special gift and because of his dark ally. A tall, lanky man of about sixty, with gray hair, a prodigious white beard, and deep-brown skin, Sabbah was, by all accounts, a formidable leader among the people. They reverently called him "the voodoo man from Iran." The black eye patch he wore over his

10

left eye—which he'd lost in his boyhood to a vicious bully who'd poked it out with a sharp stick—accentuated the aura of mystery that surrounded him.

It was that bully on the streets of Teheran who'd planted the seed of hatred in his soul so long ago, and over time that hatred fed over and over again until it nearly consumed him even before he'd turned twenty. One force in his life, the force of love, had kept that hatred at bay for a short while. It had tamped it down to a dull red ember. Once that force had been stamped out, its light nothing more than a distant memory, the hatred had roared to life and taken over, turning Sabbah into what he was now and would always be.

Sabbah took another pull on the water pipe next to him, the bubbles filling the room with a pleasant sound that heralded the comforting warmth that would soon follow as the cannabis entered his bloodstream. He breathed the fragrant smoke deeply into his lungs, and as he let out a cloud of it in the darkened room, with bamboo blinds down most of the way to cut the late-afternoon light, he glanced around the room.

Yes, he thought, *it is a simple life, with simple pleasures.*

Red candles flickered in the room, casting a strange otherworldly light that no ordinary candles could accomplish. These were special candles that opened doors to other dimensions, an arena of darkness where few men cared to roam. There wasn't much else in Sabbah's living room, just a rectangular mahogany coffee table with a couple of chairs around it, his water pipe, and an old couch with an electric floor lamp next to it. On a battered old end table was a picture of a woman wearing Western clothing. She also had on a pretty black veil, pulled back to reveal her beautiful Persian features. She had dark-almond eyes, well-defined cheekbones, and perfect white teeth. Her skin was the color of dark olives whitened with the light of the world. Her black hair was worn loose and was obviously long. Sabbah dreamily stared at the picture of the woman as he took another hit from the water pipe.

It has been so long now, he thought, *so long since her tragic death. So long since the shah's thugs took her from me.* "Oh, Suri," he whispered. "Oh, my precious Suri!"

For a moment, his stone-cold heart warmed at that thought of his late wife, and the hatred within it weakened for an instant. Then

11

the all-consuming hatred he'd lived with since her murder cascaded in its typical all-consuming fury. Even seeing the photograph of his daughter, Hannie, now nineteen, next to the one of a very young Suri, taken at a café in Teheran, did nothing to diminish the rush of violence. His breathing quickened, his hands went clammy, and he suddenly began chanting the chant of the curse he could call up on those whose futures he could foretell. He had cursed the soldiers who had killed Suri, and he had relished the visions of their gruesome deaths in the shah's torture chambers. One by one, each had been accused of treachery, dragged from his home, and taken to the cells from which no one ever emerged alive. His curse had traveled through the ether, halfway around the world from Indonesia, where he had fled with Hannie in 1953 after Suri's death in a hail of bullets.

Sabbah kept chanting, conjuring up the memory of the day he'd called the curses from deep in the fabric of evil in the world. It had happened not very far from where he was now—not very far at all, as a matter of fact. It had been on a late afternoon like this one, only during the height of the rainy season. Thunder had growled overhead as he made his way down the rocky path to an old house built on the higher ground in the Puncak Highlands. The flooding in Jakarta below had been intense, and as the waters rose, people had died. The souls of many had been set free, and Sabbah had known he could capture their power and turn it into pure energy—to bring destruction to those who had killed Suri.

Lightning had flashed and the rain come again, this time in sheets, with eddies and whirls. Gusts of wind had rattled the palm fronds and pounded on the leaves of the dense undergrowth surrounding the house. Sabbah had craned his neck to look up at the sky and had screamed, chanting the same chants the voodoo high priestess had taught him. He had taken a small basket from the canvas backpack he wore, and he had opened the lid as he stopped chanting. A snake's head had risen above the top edge of the basket. The snake had hesitated, and then it had risen higher, its yellow eyes fixing Sabbah's, its forked tongue darting in and out from between sharp fangs.

The two creatures had stared at each other as the storm raged on. Sabbah had been able to feel the souls of the dead in the flooded city below. They had come together from all over Jakarta province, converging and streaming toward him like the swollen Ciliwung River. They had gathered in a cloud in the clearing in front of the house. The cloud had pulsed and throbbed like a beating heart. The snake had opened its mouth wide, and Sabbah had watched the white wisps of human souls flowing from the brilliant-white cloud in a cylindrical pillar into the snake's mouth. Sabbah had begun chanting again as the snake dined, swelling up as more and more souls bloated its gullet.

Suddenly, Sabbah had sensed it was time. He had screamed a command in a language known only to the dark ones, and he had grabbed the snake from its basket. The snake had not struggled. Indeed, it had seemed almost to smile as Sabbah held it high. Thunder had cracked and the sky turned crimson as a horrendous had explosion echoed through the jungle. The clouds grew even redder, like the color of dark-red blood.

"At last it is done!" Sabbah had screamed. "At last it is done!"

He had lowered the snake, holding it inches from his face. The snake's tongue had flicked out, touching Sabbah's cheek.

Stirring from his memories, Sabbah took another hit from the water pipe. He smiled broadly as other visions entered his mind. These were of the near future, not the distant past when he'd first successfully summoned the power of darkness. These visions were of the people who lived all around him. He licked his lips as he saw the death of the village elder.

Soon, he thought with a smile. *Soon you will die! Your heart will bleed from inside! The pain will be superb! Soon you will die!*

Sabbah could see the stillborn baby of a young woman who had so much hope, so much love in her life. She would slit her wrists after the death of her baby. The blood would pool and coagulate. It would soak the ground and her clothes. Swarms of houseflies would lay eggs in her wounds. Her husband would wail and curse Allah. He would run into the jungle, but he would not die. Not yet. That wasn't in his future until much later. Instead, he would live with emptiness and grief that never let up.

Sabbah could also see the violence of the rebels in the surrounding jungles boiling over into bloodshed. The strife between Indonesian government forces and the religious sects in the hinterlands had simmered long enough. It was time to explode into the armed conflict that Sabbah welcomed. More souls would be set free, and that was always a good thing. He hated the government security police, the troops, and the politicians. They reminded him of the loathed shah, of the men who had killed Suri, of the bully who had jammed a stick into his eye for no other reason than to see what would happen. The bully had laughed as Sabbah's eye popped like a fat grape.

Sabbah did not need both eyes. He could see everything! Everything! Everything—except what mattered, and that was his own future. Even the dark one couldn't change that. If his gift had extended to those he loved, Suri might still be with him. It sometimes seemed that he was as cursed as those he'd taken revenge on, those he'd intimidated, those he'd killed for the sheer delight of feeding the snake! But Sabbah didn't dwell on that.

Sabbah's chanting grew louder. He leaped from his chair and began to pace in circles around the living room. Louder and louder he chanted, calling the evil in the world to him, so that he could feel its cold touch. He called the evil in his heart, and it roared out in a terrible scream that filled the air.

The telephone on the end table rang. Sabbah stopped chanting. He glared at the phone, and then he answered it.

"Yes," he said, sounding a little out of breath.

"Father?"

"Yes, Hannie?"

"Did you remember our dinner plans for tonight? I'm bringing the meal, and I'm bringing a special friend for you to meet, Father! I haven't told you about him, but it's time you met him."

"A special friend?" He was immediately suspicious. "What kind of special friend?"

"I met him through my roommate in school, Father. I'll tell you more at dinner, okay?"

"I will look forward to it," he said, but he didn't mean it. He didn't like the fact that he was hearing about a boyfriend, and he was sure that's what she meant by *special friend*, for the first time. Right out of the blue like that. But then, Hannie was always full of surprises. Her leanings to Western ways, ways of the infidels, did not sit well. A woman's place was in her home, caring for her family.

It was not out in the world where lecherous eyes could stare, where men yearned to put their penises where they did not belong, where temptations of the soul were rampant. He knew all about the way things were. The dark one had shown him that long ago.

"You'll like him," Hannie said. "You'll see!"

"Yes, daughter, we'll see," he said.

Hannie said she would arrive in about an hour, and then she hung up the phone. Sabbah replaced the receiver. He sighed. Part of him loved his daughter because she was a part of Suri, and part of him hated her for the same reason. He didn't like being reminded of his loss of Suri. He didn't like the way Hannie chose to run her life. He sat back down and relit the water pipe.

At the appointed time, Sabbah heard a vehicle approaching on the winding road leading up the low hills to his house. The engine grew louder as the vehicle got nearer, until he heard it stop in front of the house. He got up and went outside. What he saw brought him up short. Seated next to Hannie, in a military jeep, was a young man in an American uniform. It was the height of the Vietnam War and the Cold War with the Soviet Union. Americans seemed to be everywhere, and Sabbah didn't like it. He particularly didn't like his daughter fraternizing, or doing who knew what, with an American dog. His anger began to simmer right away.

Hannie got out of the jeep. Smiling, she strode toward him and said, "Father! Oh, Father, it's so good to see you!"

Sabbah stared at the young man, who had also gotten out of the jeep and was walking toward him, a big smile on his face.

"Who is this?" Sabbah asked, his voice low and cold. The infidel was unclean. He was unfit to go anywhere near Hannie. Worst of all, he was an American!

"This is James!" Hannie said. "James Parker."

His fury at learning that Hannie was apparently dating an American soldier began to gather and expand like an approaching typhoon.

James stopped in front of Sabbah and offered his hand. "Hannie has told me so much about you, sir," he said. "It's a pleasure to finally meet you!"

Sabbah surveyed the young man with reptilian coldness.

"What's the matter, Father?" Hannie asked.

Sabbah did not notice the worry on her face. He wouldn't have cared if he had.

"Sir?" James asked.

"You dare to bring an American soldier here?" Sabbah asked Hannie. "You dare to defy my wishes?"

Hannie looked down at her feet for a long moment. Then she met Sabbah's icy stare. "I dare to bring the man I love to meet my father. Yes, I dare to do that," she said. Her voice was full of defiance.

"Soldiers killed your mother."

"Not all soldiers are bad," Hannie said. "James is a good man. A good American soldier."

Sabbah could feel the rage coming. For Suri's sake, he tried to control it. "You had best be on your way," Sabbah said to the soldier. "I'll see that Hannie gets back to her dorm room."

Sabbah could see the confusion and disappointment on his face, and he was glad.

"I don't understand," James said.

"You don't have to understand," Sabbah said. "Now get out of here. *Now!*"

Sabbah noticed then the intense rage that twisted Hannie's face. Gone was the daughterly love in her eyes. Gone was her jovial mood. The anger made her look ugly. "Now you listen to me, Father," she said. "I am—"

Sabbah stepped forward and slapped her hard across her right cheek. "Show some respect for your father!"

"Hey!" James said, stepping between Sabbah and Hannie. "There's no call for that!"

The hatred was too much for Sabbah. It rose to the surface like lava. "You must never see this man again!" he shouted. "Do you hear me?"

The young couple stepped backward, giving him more room.

"Do you hear me?" Sabbah screamed. "Your hands are unclean! This man is an infidel! He is an American soldier!"

"Come on, Hannie," James said, taking Hannie's hand. "We're getting the hell out of here."

"No!" she said. She pulled away from James and stepped closer to Sabbah. She looked up at him. Sabbah could see how her eyes were pleading, begging, crying out with pain.

"I am going to have a baby," she said softly. "James and I are going to get married and have a baby."

"You slut! You mean you're pregnant?"

"Father, don't talk to me like that!" Hannie began to cry.

"You're as unclean as he is! Worse!" Sabbah shouted.

Hannie ran to James, who embraced her.

"That's quite enough," James said. "I know you are her father, but you should show her some respect. She'll be married when the baby comes. No dishonor will come to you."

"May a curse be upon you both," Sabbah said. He pointed first at James and then at his daughter. "May a curse be upon you fornicators and your unclean child!"

James balled up his right fist and raised his arm to hit Sabbah.

"No!" Hannie yelled. She grabbed James by the arm and shoved him toward the jeep. "Let's get out of here! Come on, James. Let's go."

The couple moved toward the jeep. Hannie stopped and turned to Sabbah. "I hate you, Father," she said. "I hate you for what you have said, what you are! I know what's inside you!" She was shouting now. "I know your soul is rotten and corrupt! I know that Allah no more lives in you than he does in a stone! You killed Mother! It was your fault! You killed her! It's time you admit that and stop lying to yourself and to me!"

Beyond rage now, Sabbah simply turned and walked back in the house, slamming the front door. He stood behind the closed front door and listened as the jeep's engine started up. He heard the vehicle pull away. When it had gone, he relit the candles. After he took another huge hit from the water pipe, he began chanting. The chanting grew louder and louder. And soon he was whirling in a dance as he screamed, the sounds more like the growls of an animal than of a man. The black robes he wore billowed as he turned around and around, calling the dark one to his side.

"I will feed the snake! I will feed the snake with all manner of souls!"

4

NAMES

The present, outside Montreal, Brouchard Inc., Tuesday, 1:35 a.m.

I'm making my rounds, just cruising the factory, checking to make sure doors are locked and that everything is as it should be. It seems to be, which is good, because I don't want any more excitement. I've had it, man! I'm so totally whipped, even though I slept a little earlier this evening before coming in for my shift tonight. That nightmare keeps creeping me out. Every time I round a dark corner I almost freak out. I keep seeing images of that devil face coming nose to nose with me in a roaring fire that's turning me into an overcooked version of Mannie. Stick a fork in me! I'm done!

As I make my way through the warehouse, I keep seeing those red eyes glaring at me, as if I've really pissed off the devil creature, or whatever it is. I shine my Maglite into more dark corners, and I wish to hell I could carry a piece. That's one thing about Canada that annoys me. Rent-a-cops usually aren't allowed to pack heat. So I'm walking around with my dick in my hand, and I jump at the slightest movement, even from the resident rats. The beam of my light passes over boxes and up to the steel girders overhead, and I keep seeing those yellow, gross shark teeth chomping up and down, up and down, down and up! Every once in a while, I smell Mannie as he does a bad imitation of a beef flambé, and I immediately flash back to a pig roast from my stoner days. I suddenly feel like puking all over again, but I don't actually shoot the jet.

I sigh, stifling a yawn. My mind is working overtime. *Chill, dude,* I tell myself. *Just chill, man! It's gonna be a long night as it is!*

I cruise down the hall and stop off at the assembly room. The night shift is hard at work, as usual. There's Martin, Jacques, Pierre, Tina, Chandi, Francois, Peter, and Adrian. They all glance up at me from their workstations, give me a nod of acknowledgement, and go back to their jobs. There are some other folks in there too, but I don't know their names.

"Yo, dudes! What's up?" I ask nobody in particular as I stroll on in.

"Same old crap," Jacques says.

"Yeah, Big M," Tina says, "it's like *so* boring. When am I gonna get a life? Hey, you go see Mannie today like you said?"

I pause by her station. She's a CAD chick, the one who works on creating components on this high-powered funky computer thing. She's making big bucks, whereas I'm making jack. "Yeah," I say, "I saw him."

"He doin' okay?" Tina asks.

"Suppose so. For a crispy critter."

"You're so bad," Chandi says. "That's mean."

"Yeah, Michael! Come on, man! Show the guy a little respect," Martin says. "You shouldn't dis the dude! Not after he damn near got his ball hairs fried!"

They all chime in then, razzing my sorry ass for making a joke at Mannie's expense. I say I'm sorry. They're an odd assortment of people, the night-shift assembly workers and welders. Jacques is pure Quebecois all over, preferring to speak French all the time and constantly arguing in favor of Quebec seceding from the rest of Canada. Yeah. Like that's ever gonna happen. But Jacques will go on for hours about it, if you let him, which I don't. Nobody does, in fact. He's a big guy like me, with brains to match his muscle. I like him. He's a cool dude, just the kind of guy I'd lift a few beers with any day of the week or that I'd trust to date my sister, if I had one, which I don't.

Peter and Francois are both much older, I'd say over sixty. Possibly even older, and I'm told they've been with Brouchard Inc. for decades. Peter is a little shorter than I am, with a mop of silvery hair that looks like a chicken nests in it and a frame that's muscular and yet flabby, if that's possible. Francois is a big dude, and in his younger days he must've been formidable in a bar fight.

Tina and Chandi, well, they're cute, hot brunettes with figures you get when you run a zillion miles a week and then go work out in the gym on top of that. Nothing unusual for Canadian babes. I think they're both vegans, but I'm not sure. I know they're not into each other for sex, but I also know they're really tight. Have been since college. Together, they form their own little feminine SWAT team, and they don't take crap from any of the guys.

Adrian and Martin are both built like scarecrows and have Mohawks with shades of green and purple. Their faces are augmented with enough pierce art to blow out every airport metal detector from Montreal to Mexico City. They're good guys, for the most part, except I think they're probably meth heads, at least on the weekend. I've got a nose for sniffing out misfits, especially because I am one myself, and this crew fits the bill. I've also got a nose for sniffing out people with something to hide, and I'd bet my last jelly doughnut that more than one of these mutts has a police record.

"Mannie says hello," I lie.

Jean Claude sidles over to me. "Mr. Abraham, do you think this is some kind of social hour?"

"Ah, uh—no, Jean Claude, I don't think—"

"We're not paying you to jack off in here. You check the parking lot yet?"

Jean Claude is medium height, with rusty, dark-red hair that he wears so short he could be a drill sergeant prick in the Canadian army. His white face has a parboiled patina of red from too much sun over the weekend, and his nose is peeling big time. I hope he was at the nude beach and that his ass cheeks look just as red as his ugly face. He's got a tat of a snake going up his left arm that's going to look real bad when the guy gets all wrinkly, if he lives to be an old fart, and he wears a gold cross around his neck that seems the very height of hypocrisy. Jean Claude is the last thing you'd think of as a wholesome Christian. But, hey, some of the meanest badasses in history wore crosses, so who am I to judge?

"No, Jean Claude, I haven't checked the parking lot yet," I say, rolling my eyes.

"Well, stop distracting my people, okay? Move your ass on outta here."

"Yes, sir!" I say, and give him a mock salute.

"Get out of here," he says, but I can tell he likes it when I do that, the fake salute, I mean.

I turn tail and head to the parking lot. When I get outside, I find the night air is almost chilly. It's almost always like that in Montreal during the high summer season. That is, unless the humidity from the south works its way into the St. Lawrence Valley to turn everything hot and sticky for a few days. When that happens, the living sucks, because almost nobody has air conditioners. We sweat and complain and dream about snow. We eat frosty flavored crushed ices and drink lots of alcoholic whatever. And then the jet stream does its thing and everything goes back to normal.

I take out my Maglite to shine into shadows near the loading dock. The bright orange lot lights don't reach everywhere, so it's easy to find dark places. I don't expect to see anything unusual, except maybe that devil creature again. At any moment, I think it's going to jump out from behind a dumpster and yell, "Boo!" Then I'll have to go home to get clean briefs.

I don't see anything except employee vehicles. No kids getting stoned or drinking beer in the woods that surround the property. No nothing.

"Good," I mumble and head back inside.

The night air has cleared my mind, and as I walk, I wonder about what Mannie said. Paul Brouchard is the devil. As I've said, I think that's pretty implausible. Hell, I think the whole idea of a devil creature is pretty lame. I doubt what my own eyes have seen, and yet I keep wondering if this Paul Brouchard dude has something going on that I should know about. Don't know what that could be exactly, but as the hour grows late, I begin to think maybe I might take a peek into his office just to see what I can find.

I continue my rounds, and then I go to the central offices, where the admin staff hang out answering phones, chewing gum, and talking crap about their husbands. Down a long hall past a nice conference room with wood paneling I go. I turn left and reach the executive offices. Brouchard's is the biggest one, right on the corner of the building on the south side, to get the most sunshine through the large glass windows. He's got a killer view of lots of green lawn and tall pines and not much else. Of course, when I try the knob, I find that the door is locked, but I use my master key and go right on in.

I walk quickly inside and close the door behind me as I take out my Maglite again. I rifle through the files in the wooden cabinet near Brouchard's desk, but there's nothing but financial information and other crap I don't care about. I start opening drawers in his desk, poking around here and there. Nothing. When I get to the last big drawer on the bottom, I discover it's locked. Nothing unusual about that. In fact, I'm sorta surprised any of the drawers in the file cabinet or in the desk were unlocked.

"Guess the dude's got nothin' to hide," I say. "Hmm."

I get on my knees and start feeling the bottom of the desk. I'm looking for a key, and I find one. It's amazing how stupid some people are. Like using the same four digits in a row for a password, or a birth date, or whatever. Like some burglar isn't going to look for a key taped under the desk, or a car thief for the Hide-A-Key under the rear bumper. Anyway, I grab the key, try the lock in the desk drawer, and snort in delight as the lock opens. I furrow my brow in mild confusion and totally gross out as I go through the contents of the drawer. There's a bottle of Canadian Club, a couple of joints, a can of cashews, two rubbers, a half-full jar of K-Y Jelly, and an oversize Manila envelope. There's also a box of sanitary wipes chicks use when they go camping, or for whatever.

"You bad, bad preacher boy!" I whisper, wondering if the boss has been dipping his wick in delicious Sue Young. They've probably been doing the nasty right in his office, probably right on the desk. I suddenly wish I'm wearing rubber gloves. "Delete image, man!"

Then I wonder if it's his secretary who he's doing the deed with. She's not bad looking—not as hot as Sue, but not so bad. I wonder if he's doing the deed with any of his employees. The guy's not Catholic, so he's entitled to some afternoon delight, if he can get any. I shake my head and whistle quietly as I open the envelope. I shine the Maglite on the papers to get a better look. There is a nice stack of newspaper stories held together with a spring-loaded paper clamp meant for thick bundles. I fan through them without stopping to read. *Man, there must be dozens of stories here!* I think.

Toward the end, the clips are yellow with age. At the very bottom of the pile is a story that catches my eye because of the headline and subhead. I see Brouchard's last name in it, and I check the date. The story appeared in April 1986. I scan it. It's about the gruesome murder of Paul Henri Brouchard and his wife, Evelyn, a real looker based on the photo. I assume these people were Brouchard's parents. I stop reading, my ears straining to pick up any sound of footsteps outside. I don't want to get caught in here. I glance around, pausing to listen some more. All is quiet. I go back to reading.

The ME ruled the deaths a double homicide. The initial cause of death was thought to be fire, because the house almost burned to the ground before the bodies were recovered. However, upon doing autopsies on both stiffs, the ME established that the couple had died from trauma due to dismemberment. The report included speculation that a wild animal had attacked the couple and then somehow the house had caught fire. The trauma was more consistent with a tiger mauling than with the kind of dismemberment a serial killer would resort to, but the jury was out. According to the article, Brouchard was sixteen at the time of the crime, and he evidently got tossed into the foster-care system until he turned eighteen, because no other family would or could take him.

"I'll be damned," I said. "Poor little bastard. That's rough, dude!"

I take another look at the picture of Brouchard's parents. Something's bothering me, but I don't put my finger on it right away. I check out the news clip second from the bottom of the bunch, and read another story focused on a serial rapist who was loose in the area about thirty years earlier.

Weird, man! Why keep this kinda stuff? I wonder.

I skim the third clip from the bottom of the pile. This news item deals with the hunt for a hack abortionist who evidently operated with impunity throughout the city and surrounding locale starting around 1975. Women were turning up dead because the guy didn't know what he was doing. What strikes me as interesting is that the hunt for both the doctor and the rapist stopped at around the same time that Paul Henri Brouchard and Evelyn had ended up dead.

Are these stories all connected somehow? "Humph!"

As I slide the clips back into the envelope, ready to move on to what I hope will be greener pastures, it hits me. I pull out the clip on the murders and again examine the picture of the Brouchards. Then I think of Paul. He looks nothing like his parents, and I think that's odd. *Maybe the milkman did Evelyn or something,* I think as I check my watch. It seems pretty clear that Paul wasn't their kid, at least biologically speaking, which means he must've been adopted.

I'm starting to sweat. I've been in here too long, but I keep nosing around just the same. Inside a file folder I discover a couple sheets of folded, coffee-stained, wrinkled-up yellow legal paper. I unfold them and shine the beam of the Maglite on the first page. It's a list of names. Lots of names, and I see that some of the names are familiar. Some are prominent businessmen in the city, and it hits me hard in the gut when it dawns on me that nearly every one of them is dead. I recognize the names from newspaper stories, and I immediately wonder if the pile of clips contains those same stories. Fires, car accidents, heart attacks, murders—all the causes of death were about as unnatural as you can get. I also see that some of the names on the paper are current Brouchard employees, and then I see my name at the very bottom of the page, obviously the newest addition.

"What the—"

Suddenly, the room goes as cold as ice, just as it did in Mannie's hospital room on the previous afternoon. I instantly shut the Maglite off and peer into the nearly complete darkness. The only light comes from under the door and faintly through the curtains drawn across the picture windows. I hear a skittering sound, like the nails of a big dog on ceramic tile, over on the polished granite floor by the wet bar. To my horror, I see two bright-red eyes staring directly at me, not ten feet from where I'm standing at Paul Brouchard's fancy desk.

5

SPECIAL DELIVERY

Hospital in Jakarta, Indonesia, 1970

Hannie had never felt so alone and scared in her life. Her water had broken a short time earlier in the afternoon, shocking her to no end, because she wasn't supposed to have the baby for another five weeks. She'd been studying for a law exam in her off-campus apartment when it happened, trying to carry on as if everything were normal. Of course, everything wasn't normal. Her father had disowned her, hadn't spoken to her since that terrible day. He'd cut off all her tuition going forward. James and she had gotten married a couple of days after the rift, and he had borrowed from his family to pay her tuition, but she couldn't be sure of what the future might bring. She felt certain her days at the university would be over one way or the other. James wanted to send her to live in America with his family, and she was warming to the idea.

Hannie forced herself to control her breathing. Getting carefully to her feet, she dried herself off with a towel and called the army base.

When the enlisted man on the phone answered, she told him she needed to reach Lieutenant Parker.

"He's not here. Can I take a message?"

"Get word to him right away," Hannie said, trying to speak normally. "Tell him the baby has come early! Please hurry!"

Flustered, the man said he would. "Right away! I'll find him right away!"

"Tell him to meet me at the hospital. I'm calling an ambulance when I hang up."

The ambulance arrived a short time later, and two EMTs helped her out of the apartment on a gurney, even though she protested that she could walk. Now she was speeding through downtown Jakarta. She hoped word had already reached James and that he'd be there to meet her at the ER. She didn't want him to miss the birth of his first child.

A wicked contraction had her contorting her face in pain. She screamed.

"Easy, easy now," one of the EMTs said. He was a young, clean-shaven guy, probably in his late twenties. "Breathe easy. Don't push."

"I-I-I'm trying!"

"We'll be there in a few minutes. Just hang on, okay?"

Hannie squeezed his hand in hers and closed her eyes. The siren wailed. The ambulance took a turn fast and then another. She could hear the tires race on the pavement. She felt dizzy, sick, scared, excited, sad, and even a little angry.

Why am I alone at a time like this? Why?

She felt as if she'd always been alone, ever since she'd been a little girl and had cried herself to sleep for months after the death of her mother. The abrupt departure from everything she knew—from her grandparents, from her uncles and aunts in the old country—and her complete immersion in a brand-new culture in Indonesia had made an indelible impression on her. She'd been adrift, she knew, ever since that time, gravitating to Western ways and rebelling against her Muslim upbringing and stern father.

The ambulance screeched to halt.

"Okay, Mrs. Parker, we're here. We're going to get you into the ER now," the young EMT said.

Within moments, Hannie was rushed inside. The contractions were coming closer together. The pain was excruciating. She didn't know if she could stand it. Nurses crowded around her. Looking up at them, she could see deep concern in their eyes above their surgical masks.

"Get Dr. Eid! Stat!" the head nurse yelled.

"What? What's wrong?" Hannie asked between waves of pain.

"You're bleeding," the head nurse said. "Try not to worry. Some blood is normal. The doctor will be here right away. In the meantime, we'll move you to an examining room, okay?"

Hannie nodded.

Where is James? she thought. *Where are you, my love?*

Soon Dr. Eid arrived in the examining room. He checked Hannie out and said, "Get her prepped for surgery. We'll need to do a C-section."

His voice was calm, which reassured Hannie. Another contraction hit. This one was incredibly painful. She screamed and tried to push, breathing hard and feeling sweat soak her all over.

"Don't push, Mrs. Parker," Dr. Eid said, his voice less calm. "You must try to relax."

Orderlies appeared and she was prepped for surgery.

"James," she whispered. "Oh, James, where are you?"

More contractions. More pain. She fought the urge to push, but in spite of her efforts she did what felt natural.

"It's going to be fine," the head nurse said. "You'll see. Everything will be just fine."

Hannie was more scared than anything else. She sensed that something was terribly wrong, that a malevolent darkness was taking her over from the inside out and that it would soon consume her. She'd had a strange feeling for months. It was as if there were two life forms inside her uterus, not one. She'd said nothing about her odd feelings, the double kicks, the cold sweats, or the irrational terror that had gripped her at the oddest times, like when she was in the shower or even when she was brushing her long black hair. She'd said nothing about the nightmares, those bright-red eyes, the black amorphous blob that appeared in front of her and blocked out all else.

Trembling, she reached up for the nurse's hand. "Please," she whispered. "Please call the army base. My-my husband, he's an American lieutenant. His name is James Parker."

"He doesn't know you're here?" the head nurse asked.

"I called and left a message. He should—" Hannie interrupted herself as she screamed again.

"No family? Is there anyone else we can call?"

"I have no one else here but James," she said.

"You have your baby," the head nurse said.

Hannie tried to smile, but her terror was mounting. She wanted to get up and run away. She wanted to have the pain gone and for everything to go back to the way it had been when she'd first fallen in love with James. She had been happy then. "Yes," she said, her voice barely audible. "I have my baby."

Suddenly, there was a commotion. Shouts filled the air. She could make out James's voice as he called her name.

"*Hannie!* Oh, Hannie! Let me through! Let me through! That's my wife!"

In another moment, Hannie saw James standing above her. "Oh, my darling girl," he said. "I'm here now! I'm here, my love!"

"Lieutenant, you'll have to step aside!" Dr. Eid said firmly.

"But—"

"She needs surgery immediately," the doctor said.

Hannie felt James kiss her on the lips. He held his face close to hers and said, "I love you, Hannie." And then he was gone, and she heard the swinging doors of the OR burst open as the orderlies pushed the gurney inside. The room felt cold. Very cold.

"Now, you try to relax," the anesthesiologist said. "This won't take but a minute."

As Hannie's head began to spin from the pain and the meds, she felt a stirring deep inside her, as if something dangerous and evil had awakened within her. She felt even colder.

"No," she said. "No!"

Then the world went black as the anesthesia kicked in.

Sabbah took the form of a housefly, temporarily transporting his spirit to one of the insects laying eggs in garbage behind the hospital. The dark one had shown him how to shape-shift. He did not do it often, because it required a large payment in souls for the snake. Death ran rampant everywhere in Java—everywhere in the world, in fact. The dying had run wild in China, and now death was heating up in Vietnam. Starvation and disease claimed millions in Africa. Lost souls populated the planet, but Sabbah only got credit for the ones he delivered personally to the snake.

He buzzed into the hospital, drawn to the darkness he'd spawned in his daughter. It was like a black beacon, irresistible and wonderful. He landed high on the observation window of the ER, his sticky little feet anchored firmly to the glass. He watched the surgeons and nurses frantically trying to save Hannie. The smell of blood was in the air. He could taste it, and it made him hungry.

Soon, he thought. *Soon all will be right.*

The doctor made the incision across Hannie's abdomen. Moments later, a baby boy emerged, yanked into the world from the secure warm darkness of the womb.

"We're losing her!" one of the nurses cried. She gave the blood pressure readings, which were dropping fast.

The doctor cut the umbilical cord and quickly handed the baby to a nurse, who whacked the boy on the bottom to make it cry. "Clamp!" the doctor said, working fast. "I got a bleeder!" He shouted other orders. The nurses jumped to it.

It is no use, Sabbah thought. *You can try to save her, but you will fail. You will fail!*

The frenzy continued. "Sponge! I've got another bleeder!" the doctor said, his bloody hands inside the body of the young woman.

Suddenly, the heart-monitor alarm sounded. The line went flat. "She's in defib!" a nurse cried.

The doctor grabbed the shock paddles on the crash cart and barked out the voltage setting. "Clear!"

Everyone stood back and shouted, "Clear!"

Sabbah watched as his daughter's body convulsed, rising upward and then going limp. It was a beautiful sight for him to witness. All the hatred he felt and cherished boiled and churned.

The doctor ordered his assistant to dial up more voltage. "Clear!" It was no good.

"We've lost her," one of the nurses said, her voice quiet and somber.

The doctor sighed and called time of death. Then he closed up the wound.

Sabbah rejoiced as he flew to the waiting room and watched as the infidel James broke down at the news of his wife's death. Revenge was sweet. Very sweet. As sweet as the nectar from a tropical flower in the jungle.

"I'm so sorry," the doctor said. "We did the best we could."

"And the baby?" James asked, tears streaming down his face.

"The baby is fine. Do you want to see him?"

"It's-it's a boy?"

The doctor nodded. "He's premature, as you know, but he is going to be okay."

James's face clouded. "And my wife is dead." It wasn't a question. It was a statement. Cold fury crossed James's face. He set his jaw. The life seemed to drain from his eyes.

"I'm so sorry, Lieutenant Parker. It was Allah's will, you see."

"I don't see!" James shouted. "I don't see a damn thing! The baby lives and my wife dies? Where is the justice in that? It should be the other way around!"

"Do not say that, Lieutenant! Every new life is a gift from Allah!"

James Parker glared at the doctor, clearly overcome with a wide range of emotions. The doctor said he was sorry again. "You can see your boy in a little while."

"Keep him," James said. "I want nothing more to do with him."

James stormed out of the hospital. Sabbah watched him go, celebrating a victory of sorts. Rage and negativity had won out yet again. Human beings were so predictable, so easy to manipulate. They scarcely deserved life itself, let alone any degree of happiness.

Sabbah flew into the neonatal unit and landed in an out-of-the-way place, near the top part of the wall adjacent to the door. He watched with anticipation, wondering if the creature would emerge. If it did not, it might die in the innocence of the boy. The time was critical. If it did not emerge, if it did not fight its way out into the world of filthy humanity, his efforts would have been mostly wasted. Sabbah watched the hands on the clock in the NICU move as the hours passed. At midnight, a NICU nurse came in to check the babies. There were about twelve in the unit, all of them premature and highly vulnerable.

Now! It must be now!

Sabbah almost missed it. If he hadn't had the superior vision of a fly, that first dark mist around the baby's lips might have gone unnoticed.

Ah! Come to Papa! Come to your loving Papa! Sabbah thought. He grew more excited as the mist darkened into a thick black goo and poured out of the baby's mouth. *Yes! Yes! Come to me!*

"Oh, my word!" the NICU nurse said when she saw the baby's face covered in something that looked like tar. Sabbah saw the fear in her eyes when she ran to the boy and the goo became animated, alive, pulsing with the essence of darkness. She screamed as the goo became a cloud, a dark orb so black no light shone through it. She tried to run, but the orb suddenly changed into the shape of a little devil. It was about two feet tall, and it had a pitchfork in its right hand. Its little tail swished back and forth. Its horns were tiny.

Isn't he just so cute! Sabbah crooned.

The NICU nurse was at the door of the unit when the little devil creature hurled the mini pitchfork, catching the nurse in the neck. Blood from the severed carotid artery sprayed the glass and the white wall, soaking it in crimson. The nurse collapsed, making gurgling sounds as she pressed both hands to her neck in a vain attempt to stop the fountain of blood pumping out of her body with each beat of her dying heart.

Well done, little one! Sabbah shouted in his fly head. *Great shot! Whoa!*

Then the little devil creature breathed a cloud of fire that ignited the air into an inferno. Everything burned in an instant, and Sabbah caught all the souls as they gathered above the corpses. Fire alarms sounded. As emergency personnel came running, the fire disappeared. All that remained was charred flesh, except for one baby, a little boy that the fire miraculously had not harmed.

"Get that baby out of here!" an EMT shouted, and then he puked his guts out when he saw all the dead little blackened bodies.

A nurse, crying uncontrollably, grabbed the sleeping baby and hurried from the decimated NICU.

Sabbah vanished, filling the netherworld with hideous laughter. Taking human form again, he danced for the snake under a blood-red half moon, feeding the hungry serpent the innocent souls it craved. The baby that had been spared in the fire, Hannie's dirty little slut-child, was no longer innocent now that he had given birth to his own dark one. Both were inextricably part of Sabbah's world, of the supreme dark one's domain, and the most fabulous thing about it was that the boy would never know about what lived inside him—until it was too late.

6

ENCOUNTER

The present, outside Montreal, Brouchard Inc., Tuesday, 3:10 a.m.

The beam from the Maglite does not shine through the dark form in front of me. It's as if the creature eats light, sucks it into some kind of void in space, a sort of funky other dimension that marks a door between our plane and something else I don't really want to think about at the moment. I stare the creature down. I even move toward it, wondering if I can scare it off. The thing just remains stock-still and looks frightening for a long moment, and then it starts slowly moving toward me, one step at a time. The click of its nails or claws, or whatever they are, goes silent when the creature reaches the edge of the plush carpet that covers most of the office.

"Oh, man," I say, and I step back. My butt hits the desk. The leather swivel chair rolls off to the side on the plastic carpet protector.

Now what, smart guy? I ask myself. Then I get the bright idea that I should growl at it. I try that, but it only seems to annoy the devil creature. My hands start to shake, and I almost drop the Maglite. I don't think I've ever been so cold in my life, and it gets cold in Montreal. I hear footsteps in the hallway outside, and I whirl around, taking my eyes off the devil creature for a sec.

"Son of a bitch! What now?"

When I turn back around, the devil creature is gone. *Poof!* It seems to like doing that, and I'm just as glad that it does. My heart pounds as I quickly replace the file in the bottom drawer of Brouchard's desk, lock the drawer, and duck under the desk to put the key back where I found it. The door opens while I'm under the damn desk. The light comes on. I stay still, hoping that whoever it is will go away. Probably it's Jean Claude—but what would he be doing in Brouchard's office at this hour? I see two feet in dress shoes. The shoes are attached to legs in nice dress pants. The shoes are black, and the dress pants are a deep gray—the kind of gray Brouchard wears all the time, or at least almost every time I've ever seen him, which isn't often. The legs squat, and Brouchard looks me in the eye.

"Mr. Abraham," Brouchard says, "would you mind telling me what you're doing under my desk?"

Gulp!

"Ah, uh—well, you see, Mr. Brouchard," I say, looking up at him and feeling like a fool. Brouchard stands up and steps back as I crawl out from under the desk on all fours, and then I stand up too. I put my Maglite in its belt holster. Brouchard is standing there with his arms crossed over his chest. He looks more puzzled than pissed. "I, ah, well, I thought I saw a rat! A big, hairy one!"

I know that's about as lame an excuse as my dog eating my homework, but hey, it's the only one that comes to mind. Nobody ever accused me of being a genius. That's for sure.

"A rat?"

"Yeah, a real big one," I say, going with the flow. "I thought there was a rat loose, and I was trying to track it down."

"Uh-huh."

"You see, I've been noticing all kinds of crazy things around here lately," I say, trying to change the subject. He's evidently not biting.

"You've seen big rats in my office?"

"Well, no. Guess not."

"That's what I thought, Mr. Abraham. I haven't seen any either. You know, you have that master key for safety and security reasons, but I thought Miss Young told you that this space is off limits unless there's a real emergency. She did tell you that, right?"

I nod. Gulp again! *This last twenty-four hours has been a real bitch, man!*

"Did you find it?" Brouchard asks.

"Find what?"

"Why, the rat, of course!" He actually smiles at me. He uncrosses his arms. He puts them behind his back.

"No, I didn't, sir. Ah, say, what brings you in at this hour? The early birds aren't even awake yet."

Brouchard gives me a strange look. "I actually don't know," he says.

I'm surprised. I never expected him to say that.

"You don't know why you're here? You okay, sir?"

He sighs and sits heavily down in his chair. I move away, keep a respectful distance, and pray I can get the hell out of there. I don't even care if the dude fires me at this point, though I do seriously need the cash. Yet I've about had enough of this crap. This place is creeping me out too bad, man!

"I've been having a hard time sleeping lately," Brouchard says. "Dreams. Strange dreams. I sometimes walk in my sleep. I've driven my car in my sleep. One night I woke up in front of an all-night burger stand outside of the city with fries and a chicken sandwich in my lap. I don't even like chicken sandwiches."

Oh, man, this dude's totally batty! I think, but I don't say so.

"Well, sir, you might want to get that looked at."

"I very well might, Mr. Abraham." He pauses, picks up a pen, and taps it on the desk. "What things have you seen around here? You said you've seen something. Other than big, hairy rats. What is it? I'm curious."

"I dunno," I say, "Just things. Like shadows or something. Big rats, maybe."

Brouchard actually laughs. "I don't think it was rats, Mr. Abraham." He pauses again, and his eyes get a far-off look. "Did you know people say this land is haunted?"

That throws me for a loop. "Haunted?"

"Yes," he says. "Haunted. There's an old Indian graveyard buried under the parking lot, which used to be a residence, which used to be something else way back when. People say the spirits move around at night because they want to be left alone. Maybe that's what you're seeing. I doubt it's rats, but I'll have my secretary call an exterminator, just to be sure. I'll have her do that first thing this morning when she gets in!"

"Well, ah, I guess that'd be a good idea. About the rats, I mean."

"Yes," he says, giving me a hard look. "We can't have rats here, Mr. Abraham. Rats must be exterminated immediately. There's not much you can do about ghosts, but rats? There's plenty you can do about those."

I don't like the sound of that. Is it a veiled threat? Does he know I know about his file? He'll surely move it now, what with finding me under his desk and all. And why is he being so cool about finding me under his desk? I'm starting to really think the guy is three cans short of a six pack.

"I guess I should get on with my rounds," I say. I turn to go.

"Oh, Mr. Abraham," Brouchard says. He's still tapping his pen on the shiny wooden surface of his desk. "How did you hear a rat in my office if the door was closed?"

Gotcha!

"Did I say that? No, what I meant to say was I thought I saw a rat and I wanted to check everywhere just in case it got in here. I wouldn't want it to surprise you, sir."

"Indeed," he says. He stands, walks across the office to the window, and opens the blinds. "It'll be dawn soon. I love how the light comes early in August, don't you?"

I agree. Then I leave Paul Brouchard's office and try to calm down. I haven't interacted with him more than a few times since I started working here, and that's been just fine with me. Now it's even finer. He seems really out of it. I suppose that's a good thing, because if he were tiptop in the alert department, he'd have ragged my ass right out the door after finding me under his deck with the lights off. I swear it didn't even faze him. It's as if—well, it's as if he finds people under his desk all the time!

I continue my rounds. I think about the newspaper clip on Brouchard's parents, about his time in foster care, about the abortionist nobody ever brought to justice, about the rapes and robberies, and especially about the names on the wrinkled piece of yellow legal paper. *What the hell is going on around here?* The rest of my shift goes smoothly, except I bump into Jean Claude. He sneers away at me, as always.

"I looked for you at your post. You weren't there. Where were you?"

"Looking for rats, Jean Claude."

He wrinkles up his nose, shakes his head with disdain, says something unintelligible, and stalks off like the prick he is.

I punch my time card in the clock near the break room and head into the parking lot. I light up a smoke as I get into my Toyota and fire up the engine. I know I should be tired, but the night's got me wired to the max. I'm about to drive off when I see Sue Young walking toward me in high-heel shoes, a pretty blue knee-length skirt, and a white blouse. Even at a quarter to six, it's warm enough for her to sling her pink cardigan over her left shoulder.

"You're here early!" I call to her.

She stops, smiles, and comes over to my driver's side window, leaning over a little to get more at my eye level. "Hi, Michael," she says. "Beautiful morning! The birds are singing. The sun's shining. I love it when it's warm. Reminds me of home."

I laugh, savoring her smooth Southern accent. "Well, I guess it does," I say.

"Everything go okay last night?" she asks.

"Yeah, fine," I lie. But, thinking better of it, I amble on over to a half-truth about the latest incident at the factory. "I saw Mr. Brouchard last night."

Sue looks surprised. "Really? I know he had Monday night Bible studies with his kids. Stanley and Lizzie love those times with him. He wouldn't cancel out, not unless it was an emergency. After Mrs. Brouchard died a couple years ago, he's tried to fill both roles, Mama and Papa. You know how it is."

I find this very interesting and a little sad. It seems that bad luck follows my boss around like there's no tomorrow. It must really suck for him.

"He's a widower?" I ask. "That's a shame."

"Sarah died in a fiery car wreck three years ago. It was a real tragedy. Paul—uh, Mr. Brouchard, was really devastated." Sue hesitates and then continues. "You know, he and Sarah were so happy together, especially after adopting Stanley and Lizzie seven years ago."

"They couldn't have kids of their own? Brouchard and Sarah, I mean?"

"No, I guess not."

"That's sad."

"Yeah, I suppose so," Sue says. "Stanley and Lizzie are biological siblings, so they're pretty tight. Brouchard insisted on keeping them together as brother and sister. Now isn't that just the nicest thing?"

I say nothing.

Sue shakes her head and continues, "I sometimes can't figure life out. Why such bad things happen to good people."

"I've given up trying," I say. "I just keep my belief in God strong and bank on him looking out for me."

"Uh-huh."

"You don't believe?"

"My daddy's a Baptist. Course I believe." She looks at her watch.

"I don't know that he did cancel out on his kids. I kinda doubt it," I say as I flick my cigarette out the window. Sue watches the butt tumble through the air and gets a displeased look on her face, as if she's deciding whether to say something about my being a litterbug but then decides against it.

"Why?" she asks. "Why would you say that?"

"Dunno for sure," I say. "But it was late. Real late. Like past three in the morning."

She puts her weight on one hip, making her look sexy without her even having to try. "That is late. I wonder who was watching Stanley and Lizzie?"

"He come in late often? I mean, before I started working here?"

"Well, if he does, I am not in the know about it."

I drop the bombshell. "He found me in his office."

She gives me a stern look, much worse than the one she gave me when I flicked my butt out the car window. "What were you doing in there, Michael?"

I figure I'm heading the horse off at the pass. I figure Brouchard is going to mention our encounter, and I want to prep her for it, so she's not taken off guard. It's the least I can do. I decide not to tell her he found me under his desk. Him sharing how he occasionally wakes up miles from home with chicken sandwiches he doesn't want is going to stay off Sue's radar too, at least if I can help it. And my second devil-creature sighting? Hell no! No way am I saying anything about that to anyone, with the possible exception of Mannie.

"I thought a rat got in there. That's all," I say, sticking to my story.

Sue looks alarmed. "A what?"

"A rat."

"Oh Lord!"

"Don't worry. I didn't find it," I say. I suppress a smile. She looks really freaked out.

"You didn't find it? You mean it's still in there? Loose?"

"Probably," I say, busting her balls a bit.

She stands up straight, pushes a few blonde curls away from her eyes. "You know, rat or no rat, you're not supposed to be in Mr. Brouchard's office."

"I know."

"Well, see that it doesn't happen again."

"It won't," I say. "Just thought you should know in case you get subjected to the Spanish Inquisition."

"That's what I'm going to get, no doubt. The real third degree." Sue sighs. "And this was starting off to be such a nice day." She sighs again and says, "Well, you'd best get on home. Get some sleep."

I say I will, tell her to have a peachy day, and drive off.

7

CONFESSION

The present, Montreal, hospital burn unit, Tuesday, 7:32 a.m.

Instead of driving home, I grab a cup of coffee and an egg croissant at a little café near the hospital and stop to think things over. I decide it's not up to me to play the role of detective, that all I'm asking for is trouble, and it isn't worth the hassle for thirteen bucks an hour. But as I munch, I also think it's been pretty exciting at work lately and that I haven't had this much adventure in a long time, at least not in my adult life. So I figure it's cool if I poke around a little more. What the hell? You only live once. Besides, how often do you get to do the tango with a devil creature?

After breakfast, I head back to the hospital to visit Mannie. I have questions. Once I'm at his side, I just sit looking at him. The poor guy is in a bad way. The attending nurse tells me he took a turn for the worse before I came in. Something about an infection and lots of pus, which doesn't sound good. Not good at all. It actually sounds kinda gross, the pus part, anyway.

"You can see him but only for a few minutes," the nurse said. "I mean it. The only reason I'm letting you in at all is you're the only person who's come to see him. I mean, nobody's even sent a card! No flowers either. Can you believe that?"

I thanked her, thinking what a crime it is to be alone on your probable death bed.

Now I'm sipping a coffee-to-go in an uncomfortable chair pulled up next to Mannie, and I'm debating about where I should poke him to see if he's done yet. I want to wake his ass up. It occurs to me that out of everyone at the company I've only gotten to know Sue Young, and I don't even know her well, but I've been getting to know Mannie. It feels good, in a way. Everybody else at work just minds their own business, which is normal, I guess, but at my other security jobs I've always been like the resident bartender. People tell me things. Nobody has said jack at Brouchard Inc., and that strikes me as a little off.

"Hey, Mannie," I say at normal volume level, hoping I'll jog his brain out of its dormancy. "Dude, man, wake up! It's time to make the doughnuts!"

Mannie stirs just a little. They've got the poor guy tied down so he doesn't rip off the skin grafts, but he can still move a little. He opens one eye and then the other. He smiles at me, and I can see he's genuinely pleased I'm here.

"Hey," he says, his voice raspy, "good to see you back, man! What's up?"

"You okay?"

"No, not really, but thanks for asking." Mannie coughs and asks for a drink of water.

I see the nurse has set a cup of ice cubes near his bed. How he's supposed to reach them when he's all lashed down is beyond me, but who am I to reason things out about health care? I push the bed button to raise Mannie into a sitting position and feed him an ice cube to suck on. "That better?"

"Yeah, man!" He sucks for a little bit. "What are you doin' here, Michael?"

"I'm worried about you," I say.

"You should be," he says, and then he starts coughing. "I feel like shit, man!"

"I'm sorry."

"So am I."

I take another sip of my coffee. Mannie sucks on his ice cube. We sit in brotherly communion for a few long moments. Then I say, "You know, I saw the devil creature again last night."

Mannie doesn't say anything, keeps sucking his ice. But his eyes look afraid again, like they were yesterday when the devil creature showed up in his room and scared both of us until we about peed our briefs.

"You did?" he asks.

I nod.

"What did it do?" Mannie asks.

"Nothing."

Mannie laughs. "Nothing? You kiddin'?"

"No, seriously! It just stood there looking like an ugly-ass creature from hell, flipping its tail, gnashing its fangs, staring at me with those freakin' big red eyeballs, and then it disappeared when Brouchard walked in like the dark horse he is."

Mannie looks confused. "What?" he asks.

"Sorry," I say. "It's like, well, I was under Brouchard's desk and—"

"You were where, man? Sorry, buddy! I thought you said you were under Brouchard's desk!"

"Let me back up," I say. I fill Mannie in on everything.

"I told you," Mannie says, a triumphant look in his eyes. He even smiles. "I told you our boss is the devil!"

"I think everybody thinks their boss is the devil, Mannie," I say, but I'm starting to believe it too. There's too much hinky crap goin' down for a situation-as-normal kind of thing. I tell myself it can't be true, but I'm not so sure about anything anymore.

"Not like this, man!" Mannie says. "Our boss is the real thing. The real Devil Dog!"

"Maybe," I say. "But I've never liked devil dogs. Too sweet."

Mannie groans, and I don't blame him. I start to repeat the business about what I found in the file, but Mannie interrupts me.

"What time did you see it?"

I think back and tell him it was a little after three o'clock.

"I saw it at about two fifteen, I think," Mannie says. "Can't be sure. I was screaming my head off at the time, and then the nurses all came running in and gave me something. But I think it was about that time."

I say nothing, but my mind is buzzing as if it's full of irritated bees. Nothing is clicking, though, except it worries me that the creature made an appearance in Mannie's room. It bothers me that it vanished and then appeared at Brouchard's factory while I was nosing around. The time difference between sightings seems significant somehow. I get back to what I was saying. I tell him, "I think the stories in that file are all connected, but I can't figure it out. And why are some of our names on that list? It's just too weird, man. Too weird!"

Mannie goes quiet. He closes his eyes.

"Mannie? You asleep?"

"No, asshole," he says, his voice sounding suddenly sad. "No, I'm not sleeping. Wish I were. Gimme another ice cube, will ya?"

I comply. I wait for him to suck some more and to continue speaking, which he does.

"Everything's not as it seems," Mannie says.

"No shit, Sherlock," I say.

"We both see the devil creature. That's just not right, man. It must mean something. Maybe we've pissed it off or something. Anyway, I've heard things about people at work. The employees. Were all the employees on that list?"

"How should I know? It's a big company," I say, feeling a bit exasperated. I finish my coffee and squish the Styrofoam cup. I look around for a trashcan, spot one, get up, and toss the cup in.

"Some of us aren't as white as the driven snow, you know," Mannie says.

"Who is?" I say, sitting down again. "I know I'm sure not. Dogs piss on the snow wherever I go. So everything's a little yellow. Or a bus goes by and splashes slush on my shoes. Gets me all wet and dirty. That's life, man! Wet and dirty." I sigh. "Look, I'm just filling you in on what I've found out. Figured you'd like to know. I thought maybe you'd have some insights."

"Sure, Michael," he says. He closes his eyes again.

"Dude, if you're gonna sleep, I better go get some shut-eye myself. My shift starts at nine o'clock tonight." I get up.

Mannie opens his eyes, swallows hard. "Stay, Michael," he says. "I have something to say. Really."

I sit down. I say nothing.

"I've got a past I'm ashamed of, something that's haunted me for a long time. When—"

"Come on, Mannie," I say. "Now's not the time for this. No sense in wallowing in the past, right?"

"Shut up, will ya? This is hard enough as it is, and I'm trusting you, man! Really trusting! So, anyhow, I grew up in Morocco. Did you know that?"

I shake my head.

"Life wasn't easy for a Jew there."

I'm surprised that Mannie is Jewish. He's never said. But I keep my mouth shut.

"I killed a man, Michael. A scumbag drug dealer, but I bagged him and grabbed the loot. I ran away as fast as my sorry ass would go. I snuck into America, and then, like a *schlemiel*, I lost the fortune in Las Vegas at the craps table."

"Come on," I say, "you're bullshitting, right? You lost your shirt at craps? Man! What kind of a moron are you?"

Mannie shakes his head. He tries to laugh, but I can see it hurts. He stops trying to laugh. His face gets serious again.

"Even if you're not delirious, what does this have to do with anything?" I ask.

"Because Sue Young knew my background was fake when she hired me. She told me she knew I was bullshitting on my application. She doesn't know about what happened back in Morocco or anything, but she knows I got into Canada with false papers. When I asked her how she knew, she just smiled and told me not to worry about it. When I asked her why Brouchard hired me anyway, she just said he believed in second chances. Him being a reverend and all. You believe that? Second chances? Second chances for what? To end up in the slammer?"

"I still don't get it, man," I say.

"Don't you see? Brouchard is collecting people like me. We all have something to hide, I'm sure of it. We all are damaged goods in some way. I can't say for sure, but I think it's true, Michael! I can feel it in my guts! And so I want to know what your secret is. What did you do to end up on that list?"

Mannie's question hits me like a Louisville slugger. Right smack in the head. Sure, I have secrets. Some of them aren't nice. Some of them are downright nasty, and I don't like to dwell on them. Now I'm starting to wonder if my getting involved in all this is just a coincidence or if it's by some demonic grand design. The very notion of it makes me feel uncomfortable.

"I'm as pure as the driven snow, man," I say.

"You just said dogs piss on you."

"I lied."

"Sure," Mannie says. "You're an asshole, you know that?"

"So I've been told."

Mannie moans. I press his morphine drip. He seems to feel better.

"You look into the other employees, including Sue Young, and you'll see! I know you will!" Mannie says, his voice revealing some excitement that wasn't there before. He seems to have forgotten his question about my secrets, and I'm fine with that.

"Are you seriously saying you offed somebody, Mannie?" I ask, circling back to where we had started on this whole wild goose chase.

Mannie nods.

"Son of a bitch," I whisper.

"Ah, you promise you won't say anything? If I ever get out of here, which is doubtful, I don't want the po-po after me!"

"I'm not sure I can do that," I say. "I'm not sure I can keep quiet about a murder. Even if it was a scumbag drug dealer like you say."

"Sure you can. Just don't say anything. Forget a little birdie whispered in your ear."

"It's not that simple."

"Yeah, it is. Don't be a self-righteous prick," Mannie says. "It was a long time ago. The guy deserved to die. I'm dying anyway. What's the—"

"You're not dying," I say, feeling upset that he really might die. I'm starting to acknowledge that for the first time. "You're gonna be fine," I lie. I'm lying a lot, and I don't like it.

Mannie's eyes are suddenly wide with fear. He seems to have left the building, at least figuratively. "I saw it coming for me," he says. "The devil creature. It was terrible. Its yellow teeth were chomping and snapping, and then the thing went away, just like that. But I thought for sure I was a goner, man," he says. "It was, how do you say? Rad, man! Real rad!"

"Busy little bugger, isn't he—the devil creature, I mean," I say. My head is still spinning from Mannie's confession.

Mannie keeps sucking on the ice cube, and then he starts chewing it. I hear it crunching loudly as his molars grind the ice into little bits. "Well, anyway, that monster'll get me sooner rather than later," Mannie says. "If it doesn't, the infection will, so do me a favor and keep your mouth shut about what I said, okay? Can you do that for me? I know we're not really tight, but I'd like to think you're a friend. So can you keep your lips sealed about what I just told you?"

I nod, reluctantly.

A look of relief crosses Mannie's face. "Gimme another ice cube, Michael. I'm parched."

I give him another ice cube.

He starts chewing it. "You know? You know you should quit, right? Like all the rest of 'em?" Mannie asks.

I can see he's getting tired. His ice cubes are almost gone, and I don't feel like calling the nurse to get more. "What do you mean by that?" I ask.

"Just like I just said, man! You should quit like the rest of 'em. Sue has been trying for months to get a security guard to stay on, and they all quit after a night or two on the job, until you showed up. Frankly, we've all been amazed you've stuck around for this long."

"I had no idea," I say.

Mannie laughs weakly. "Of course you had no idea! We had a pool on you as to when you'd pull out. I told everybody they could trust you because you're a Valley Boy at heart. Am I right?"

"Go to hell, Mannie," I say, and I get up to leave.

"I'm already in hell, my friend," he says. "I'm already in hell with a devil dog."

"Woof!"

"Very funny," Mannie says.

"Glad you think so."

I tell him goodbye, and as I leave, I'm wondering if he isn't right, that life on this earth is just one form of hell. Maybe I should practice Hinduism instead of Judaism. Then I'd get more than nine lives, like the cats that live over me in the apartment upstairs. Hell, though, with my luck I'd come back as a goldfish or a garden slug or a turkey vulture. No sleek cougar. No graceful dolphin. Just a slug some bird would eat the first chance it got, or I'd end up squashed on the sidewalk under some dude's shoe. Come to think of it, that's how most of us end up—mashed potato under the rich man's heel.

With that depressing thought, I walk slowly back to my car, lighting a smoke on the way. As I'm pulling out of the parking lot, I could swear that I see Brouchard pulling in. I take off my shades, but the car is gone, lost in the zillions of others milling around.

"You're just seeing things," I say. "Dude, you got to get some sleep, man!"

8

SLAIN

The present, downtown Montreal, Tuesday, late morning

As tired as I am, I make one more stop before heading home for some sack time. I cruise over to the home office, park, and stroll into my boss's lair. Laurent Barra is a decent enough guy, and I've worked for him as a temp rent-a-cop for a couple of years now. He could be Danny DeVito's twin—besides the fact that he's built like Arnold Schwarzenegger. His door is open, so I go right in after giving the doorframe an obligatory knock. I find him hunched over reading some paperwork, a scowl on his face. I cough to get his attention. He looks up. The scowl disappears, and he gives me a smile.

"Michael!"

"Hey, Laurent," I say.

"What's going on?" he asks. "I thought you worked last night. You should be in bed."

"I know," I say, "but we need to talk."

"Sit down," Laurent says, gesturing to one of the chairs in front of his desk.

I comply.

The morning sunlight fills the small, cluttered room. There are pictures of his wife and kids and floppy-eared mutt on the wall next to some weird floral print from an obscure artist who probably shouldn't have quit his day job. Outside Laurent's inner sanctum I hear phones ringing and fingers tapping away on keyboards. It's the sound of work, that day-to-day thing we all gotta get through somehow. I sit down and lean forward a little.

"Laurent, things are kind of funky at Brouchard Inc."

He furrows his brow. The corners of his mouth turn down. He's not quite frowning, but getting close. "Funky how?" he asks.

I couch the truth a tad, leaving out the devil creature and the fact that I broke into Brouchard's office. Laurent will think I'm nuts about the creature, and he'll probably fire my ass if I say I took a sneak peek in a client's private office in the middle of a shift. Instead, I build up the idea that there's some kind of corporate espionage going on that's designed to sabotage the business. "I'm not sure Mannie's injury was really an accident," I say. "It just doesn't feel right."

"Why not go to the boss with this?" Laurent asks, leaning back in his chair and folding his hands behind his balding head.

"Because I think Paul Brouchard might be hiding something as well. He could even be behind what's going on. You know. For an insurance payoff for business interruption or something else."

"I'm skeptical about that, but okay. I'll bite. So what does this have to do with the agency?"

"Can you run background checks on these people?" I hand Laurent a list containing the names of Brouchard, Sue, Jean Claude, and Mannie.

"This is highly irregular, Michael," he says.

"Yeah, I know, but if we can come up with something, it could bring in a good fee if Brouchard is clean and he's ending up on the short end of the stick from a corporate espionage point of view. He'll pay for more of our services, I'm sure. And if he's dirty, then don't you want to know? At the very least, we should know from an agency liability perspective."

Laurent thinks things over for a long moment. I fidget in my chair, stifle a yawn, and think about the sandman.

"Okay, Michael," he says, putting the list down. "I can put a geek on it for an hour or two, but no more. And the only reason I'm doing this is because I like you. You've got the instincts of a good PI, as I've said. Let's see if you're onto something. Might be interesting."

I say thanks and stand up.

"I'm saying you should get your license. I could put you right to work on that side of the business. Say for fifty thou to start," he says.

Laurent Barra has made this offer to me before, and every time he has I've fobbed it off. But I know I'm not getting any younger. I know that life seems to be passing me by, so this time I'm not so quick to say no. "Let me think on it, okay, boss?"

He says that's fine, and we both say goodbye.

Outside, the sky has gone a little cloudy. The air smacks of humidity, and I can feel thunderstorms just over the horizon.

Paul Brouchard pulls into the parking lot and parks his Cadillac Escalade in an open space. He doesn't get out of the vehicle. Instead, he sits there, his mind going over the events of the last month, most particularly the fire that almost killed one of his employees. Somehow he feels out of place, as if something isn't right, and he can't put his finger on it. All he knows is that his sleep has been more disturbed than ever, and he has a feeling of impending doom he can't shake. Even Stanley and Lizzie have picked up on it. At eleven and nine respectively, his kids are attuned to his moods more than anyone else in the world. That has been even more the case since Sarah's tragic death.

The nightmares are vivid and frightening, and he can't help replaying them in his mind as he sits in his SUV watching life go by, his eyes dull and his heart beating faster than it should. He keeps seeing a strange bearded man in flowing black robes dancing under a blood-red crescent moon in some faraway jungle clearing. He's chanting as he twists and pirouettes. And when he turns his face skyward, it's clear that he's wearing an eye patch. Then he seems to float into the air, coming closer and closer. He's laughing and pointing accusingly. He screams, and suddenly a snake with blazing eyes rises up out of a basket. The man and the snake kiss. That's usually when Brouchard lurches awake, soaked in a cold sweat and feeling totally grossed out.

These dreams differ from the ones that have plagued him for most of his life. Like the one where flames surround and burn row after row of marching babies, all screaming in agony as they walk through the inferno like so many little soldiers in diapers. He has talked about these horrifying images with his therapist, but no amount of psychological digging has turned up the origins of these nightmares. The very real images of the death of his adoptive parents when he was sixteen could more easily be explained, except for the strange appearance of a devil-like creature in his dreams. He dreams of the creature ripping his mother's arm off and eating it, blood gushing from the stump as she screams, blood smearing the monster's horrible face, its sharp teeth red with gore. He dreams of his father walking slowly in circles in the master bedroom with a pitchfork sticking out of his forehead. In the horror of the nightmare, his father turns to him and points an accusing finger.

"This is all your fault, son! Why have you killed us? Why? We gave you love! We gave you a home when no one else would!"

Then the screams of both parents merge into a keening so wild and primitive it always awakens Paul, who is usually screaming as well. He has soundproofed his bedroom to keep from waking the kids up in the middle of the night. That's how frequent his nightmares are, and they're becoming more frequent. His therapist has said that his finding the corpses of his parents, and then the subsequent fire that engulfed them, has traumatized him. Paul guesses that is true enough. He's never gotten over the loss. He's faced so much loss in his lifetime.

"A boy should not have to see such things," the therapist said. "It is beyond the scope of our ability to emotionally handle the consequences. It's no wonder that you have trouble sleeping and connecting with other people. But there's hope. There's always hope, with lots of hard work and will power."

"I keep seeing the firemen running out of the house and then doubling over to puke their guts out. They said a monster had come to our home and chowed down on Mom and Dad. They said they'd never seen anything so gnarly before in their lives," Paul continued. "The fire was put out, but not before it cooked the bodies real good. What was left of the house was torn down after that."

The burdens began after the death of Paul's adoptive parents. The purgatory of foster care, the unrelenting drive to succeed in business, his divergence from the pursuit of money to marry and become a preacher, it all had come together to shape the man he is now.

He sighs and rubs his eyes.

"Get hold of yourself!" he whispers. "You're okay. You're okay," he repeats over and over again. "Lord, hear me! Bring comfort to my soul!"

His mind wanders to the nocturnal forays when he finds himself in his SUV far from home in the middle of the night. He had done it again earlier in the morning; he'd awakened right here in the hospital parking lot. He'd been confused and frightened, though he knew it was only his usual sleepwalking, or—more appropriately—sleep driving. When he came to, he'd felt out of control, as if he were not in charge of his own thoughts or movements. He'd begun to drive home when he felt the irresistible urge to go to the office.

What is happening to me? he wonders.

He has felt a force since early this morning that drew him first to the hospital, next to work, and now back here. He suddenly feels very tired, more tired than he has ever felt before.

I'll close my eyes for just a few minutes, he thinks. *Just a few minutes of rest will be good.*

Sabbah, his corporeal spirit having taken again the form of a housefly, buzzes between the automatic doors in the hospital lobby, coming in right behind an elderly couple with walkers. The slow movers give him ample opportunity to get in without getting squashed or swatted. He flies high along the ceiling, avoiding the heat of the overhead lights, and then up into the ventilation system. There's disgusting black mold, clumps of gray dust balls, and gauzy cobwebs in the ducts, which might trap him if he's not careful. It's almost completely dark, but that's fine. He doesn't need sight to navigate. He's drawn to Mannie, whose soul stinks of death. The lovely odor draws Sabbah hungrily on, anxious to witness the scum's final end at the hands—or teeth—of his creation.

A few minutes later, Sabbah emerges from the vent in Mannie's room. He lands right on Mannie's nose, noting that the fat man can't move his arms because of the restraints in place to keep him immobile while he heals. Mannie moves his head back and forth, but Sabbah stays put. Slowly, Sabbah inches down the nose, and then he walks along and sits on Mannie's eyelid. The man blinks rapidly, scooting Sabbah off.

"Get off you stupid fly! Get off and stay off!"

Sabbah laughs hysterically. *You dumb ass,* he thinks. *If you think a fly dance is a pain in the butt, then just wait to see what happens to you next!*

Sabbah goes in under a loose fold of a bandage and buries his fly mouth in the moist dead skin. The taste of blood and pus turn him on! Now the man is screaming! A nurse rushes in.

"F-f-f-fly!" Mannie yells. "It's inside my face! My freakin' face, man!"

"Shhh! Now calm down," the nurse says.

"Fly!"

"What fly?" the nurse asks. "I don't see a fly."

"It's eating me! It's laying eggs in my head! I'm gonna have maggots living in my head! Yucky wriggling white wormy worms living in my fuckin' head!"

Sabbah continues burrowing into the wounds, loving every minute of it.

"Now, now, there," the nurse says. "Your mind is playing tricks on you. I'll give you something to make you sleep."

"No! Get it off me! Get it off!"

The nurse injects a sedative into Mannie's IV. "You'll be out like a light in no time," she says, patting him on the head as if he were a puppy or a cute little kid.

"No, no!"

Sabbah sees the nurse leave. He feels Mannie's breathing slow as the sedative kicks in. Soon the man is snoring. *Almost time!* Sabbah thinks. *It's almost time for the fun to begin!*

9

SURPRISE!

The present, outside Montreal, Brouchard Inc., Tuesday, night shift

I'm driving out of the city on my way to work after a crappy afternoon's sleep. My eyes are bloodshot, my joints are sore, and I'm still hungry because a boil-in-the-bag dinner of Swedish meatballs just hasn't hit the spot. The road meanders through fields and woodlands, and the sun is low on the horizon. It's peeping out between massive thunderheads to the west, and I know we're in for a storm tonight. I'm not thinking about much until a newsflash on the radio brings me up short. Real short, which isn't easy to do, I can tell you that!

"Son of a bitch," I say as I listen.

The newscaster is describing a gruesome incident in Montreal's premier burn unit. My heart sinks. I grip the steering wheel tight. *Mannie, it's got to be Mannie!* I think. *That damned devil creature got Mannie!*

The details are sketchy, but according to the police spokeswoman that the newscaster cites in the report, at about ten thirty that morning a fire inexplicably broke out in a private room in the burn unit, causing the evacuation of the entire hospital for about two hours. When first responders arrived on the scene, they found the burnt corpse of a victim who had been injured in a freak industrial fire several weeks earlier.

"The victim's name is being withheld pending notification of next of kin," the newscaster says.

"Good luck with that," I say. "Mannie's a ghost for real now." I try to relax my grip on the wheel, but I'm wound up tight. I'm not surprised to hear that the ME has ruled the death a homicide. The newscaster goes on to quote a fireman as saying the room "looked like a slaughterhouse." The victim had apparently been partially eaten before being burned in the fire.

"Eaten? Oh, man!" I say, shaking my head. I can scarcely believe my ears. I tell myself it can't be true, that the report has to be some kind of sick joke, but deep down I know it's real.

"Yahweh, have mercy on that poor man's soul," I say. "Forgive him for his sins. I think he was truly repentant."

I switch the radio off and drive on in silence. I light a smoke and take a big drag. The warm summer air, the beautiful scenery, the faint tinges of orange against the thunderclouds as the sun begins to set, it's all so apart from the scurry and tangle of human existence. It's all so peaceful, even with a summer storm coming. I feel anything but peaceful, though. I feel angry and sad at the same time.

"You were a good dude, Mannie," I say quietly. "A good man in spite of your past."

I take another drag, keeping my eyes on the road. Deer live in these woods, and I don't want any unpleasant surprises coming to visit through my windshield. My cell rings. I answer it. "Yeah?"

"Is that any way to greet a boss bearing gifts?"

"Oh. Hi, Laurent," I say. "What's up?"

"Have you heard the news? Your guy, right?"

"Just now, and yeah. I'm sure it's Mannie."

"That's rough, Michael. I'm sorry. I know you liked him."

"Yeah, I actually did. Didn't know him very well, but he was okay, you know?"

I ease into a turn and hang a right onto the access road that leads to Brouchard Inc. Ever since I started working at the company I've wondered why it is located so far out in the middle of nowhere. The drive from the city is long, and if I didn't need the money so much I'd have canned this gig right from the beginning, like so many other guards before me. A clap of thunder rips through the air. I see a flash of lightning.

"This is just too weird, man," I say, dragging heavily on the butt.

"The cops are still investigating."

"I'm sure they are," I say. "I bet they don't find anything either."

"Look, I'm still at the office and Sophie is going to kill me as it is, because dinner is probably ruined. So I gotta make this fast. Well, I had the geeks look around. Like I said," Laurent says.

"And?"

"Brouchard is squeaky clean. His congregation gives him good marks. He pays his taxes, as far as we can tell. No criminal record. No debts beyond the usual. No offshore bank accounts."

"Okay, I get it! The guy's Snow White."

"Uh-huh," Laurent says. "We did establish that he was adopted when he was just a couple months old. The papers are officially sealed, but we were still able to go through back channels to track down the fact that the adoption originated here and that the baby was born in Jakarta. The mother died in childbirth, and the father, an American soldier, put the kid up for adoption. As you know, that kind thing happened a lot with so many Americans deployed in Asia during the Vietnam War."

"I'll be damned," I say, momentarily forgetting about Mannie. "Brouchard's past gets even more interesting."

"There's more. On the day Paul Brouchard was born, like ten babies in the NICU with him burned to death from a mysterious fire, and there was a murder. The NICU nurse was brutally stabbed multiple times, and it wasn't a knife. The forensics unit in Jakarta never determined what the murder weapon was. We got all that from press reports. Pay dirt, really. Except I don't know what it all means."

I'm so shocked I almost drive into a tree. I never did like coincidences, and I surely don't like this one. "She wasn't eaten was she? The NICU nurse?"

Laurent laughs. "No, Michael, she wasn't eaten. Just stabbed and grilled."

"Yeah. Like that. Kinda like poor Mannie."

"Sort of, I guess."

"How did Brouchard survive?" I ask. "If other babies burned up, why didn't he?"

"People at the scene are quoted as saying it was a miracle," Laurent says. "Like the fire spared him on purpose or something. Weird, right?"

"Way weird. You get anything on the others?" I ask.

"Mannie's an interesting case. He sort of just appears. He's—uh, *was* something of a ghost. His paper trail only goes back seven years. Sue is clean as a whistle. And this Jean Claude you love so much was one of the unlucky few in the military to serve as an exchange officer in Iraq, doing his time with the Yanks. He even saw a little combat while he was over there."

"Humph," I say. I'd figured Jean Claude had a military background. Something in the way he carries himself.

"That's about it on him. He was honorably discharged two years ago. He's worked for Brouchard ever since."

"Okay," I say.

"You keep nosing around, if you like. This murdered employee's got my antennas twitching," Laurent says. "I think you're right. There *is* something funky going on at that place."

"Glad you agree, man," I say.

I pull into the factory parking lot and find a spot near the entrance to the building. Big drops of rain begin to pelt my windshield, and I roll the window almost all the way up to keep from getting soaked, exhaling a cloud of gray smoke out the crack while I'm at it. Lightning illuminates the sky, and thunder growls louder. I thank Laurent and hit End to finish the call. I sit in the car looking at the approaching storm. *So Mannie was probably telling the truth,* I think. If his past only dates back seven years, then he probably really did sneak into the country on false creds, and that means he probably really did croak that drug dealer he was talking about. The one in Morocco.

"Hmm." And Brouchard. Now, there's a real interesting case. He survives a fire as a newborn infant. His mom dies in childbirth, and his dad hangs him out to dry. His adoptive parents are gnawed and barbecued. His wife goes up in smoke in a car wreck. And now one of his employees dies just as his adoptive parents did. I mean, man, the dude is bad news! Or dangerous. Or both.

I contemplate the stack of newspaper clips I found in that file, the ones about a rapist and an abortionist from a zillion freakin' years ago, and I wonder how these fit into the puzzle. How do all those news stories fit in? Then I consider the list, the one with my name on it. Many of the men and women whose names I recognize were under investigation for a whole bucketful of alleged crimes. I flick my cigarette out the window even though I know Sue would get pissed off if she were around. It hisses as it goes out on the increasingly wet pavement. I close the window all the way, get out of the car, and lock the doors before hurrying into the building. I'm immediately struck by the fact that nobody's on station in the lobby.

Where's the day shift guy? I wonder.

"Hello?" I call out as I head to the time clock near the break room. "Anybody home?"

It's oddly silent, except for the thunder, which seems to be getting closer every minute. I don't hear machines thumping, cutting, and humming. I don't hear radios or voices. In fact, I don't hear a solitary thing except for the storm outside. Rain patters on the metal roof. I punch in and grab my gear, such as it is. As I'm turning to head down the hall, I hear a familiar voice behind me.

"You're late," Jean Claude says.

"No, I'm not."

Jean Claude points to his watch, holds it up for me to see. "Yeah, you are."

"Oh, come on! I'm only like five minutes late," I say as I turn to go.

"We're having a prayer meeting in the assembly room," Jean Claude says. "For the night shift. For Mannie. Sue's there. So are some of the others from the executive suite."

"That so?"

"Yeah, the boss says everyone on the night shift has to be there. Sent me to get you before you started your rounds," Jean Claude says. He crosses his arms on his chest, causing his biceps to bulge out. He taps his right foot to show me his impatience.

"I'm Jewish," I say. "I don't do Christian prayer meetings."

"Don't matter. Brouchard wants everyone there. That means you, douche bag."

"Okay then," I say. "No need to get uppity about it. Lead on, dude!"

We walk together through the admin section of the building, and in a few minutes we're in the warehouse. The thunder grows louder. The rain drumming on the roof sounds like all the fingers in heaven tapping on the steel.

"You liked Mannie, didn't you?" Jean Claude asks as we reach the middle of the warehouse.

I just nod.

"Lots of us liked him," Jean Claude continues. "Shame he's dead."

"Yeah, man, a real shame," I say.

We're almost to the other side of the warehouse when I spot a foot wearing a sneaker jutting out from behind a rack packed with metal parts.

"Yo," I whisper, pointing, "check it out, dude!"

Jean Claude's eyes travel down the length of my arm, down the tip of my right index finger, and along the sight line to the mysterious foot.

"Shit," he says.

We both hurry over to the foot, and when we round the corner of the rack, we find the foot is attached to a leg. There are two legs, in fact, and both are attached to a bloody body with two arms folded neatly on its chest like you see at wakes.

"Fuck me!" I scream.

"Holy shit!" Jean Claude shouts. "What the fuck happened to the head?"

"Dunno!" I say, my voice still loud but coming down a notch.

"Maybe we should go look for it!" Jean Claude says, his voice also coming down a notch.

Neither of us move. We're both hyperventilating a little and are in a bit of shock at the horrific and unexpected sight. We stand there, staring at the corpse, unsure of what else to say. A lake of fresh blood has pooled around the body, covering the gray concrete floor in a slick that's starting to look real sticky and super gross. It's not a little lake either. We got Lake fuckin' Superior going on here. Big time!

"Man, I saw this kinda shit in Iraq. IEDs, you know?" Jean Claude says. "Never thought I'd see it here."

I give him a look that says, *You got that right!* I kneel down and try to read the nametag on the uniform while trying not to hurl my Swedish meatballs or look at the stump of the neck with a chewed up spear of spine sticking out. It looks like someone or something gnawed the head right off. There are all kinds of stringy white ligaments or something all over the place, along with big gnarly veins and some black crap I can't identify. I'm thinking of the devil creature again as I take my index finger and gently rub blood from the cotton embroidered nametag. It identifies Peter Galipo, one of the older guys on the staff. I stand up again, wipe my bloody finger on my jeans.

"Man," Jean Claude says, now able to read the nametag himself. "Peter!"

"Yeah, it's Peter. We got to call the cops! Someone's chopped the dude's head off, man! Where the fuck is the head?"

"How do you know it's even Peter? Just because the guy's got Peter's uniform on doesn't mean it's really Peter."

"Good point. Well, the head's gotta be around here somewhere!"

"You sure about that?" Jean Claude asks.

"Hell, no! I'm not sure about anything!" I take out my cell to dial 911. "You go tell Mr. Brouchard what's happened, okay? Tell him the cops are en route. I'll stay with the body."

Jean Claude says fine and runs off. I hear the steel door close with an ominous clang, and then I'm alone with the DB and the storm. The humming fluorescent lights make the scene even more ghastly. I'm so totally creeped out I'm trembling as I press 911 and the call goes through.

"I want to report a murder," I tell the nice calm dispatcher lady.

"What is your location?"

I give her the information and the particulars of the scene. She says to stay put and not touch anything. She asks if the killer is still around. I say I hope not.

Knowing the cops are on the way, I feel a little better, though not much. I cruise around looking for the head. *If I were a head, where would I be?*

"Here head," I say in a singsong voice. "Here little head! Here little head, head, heady! Come out, come out, wherever you are!"

You're a sick dude, you know that? I tell myself, and I have to agree with the little scolding voice in my own very-much-still-attached head.

I notice blood spatters leading down the aisle. Big blotchy red splat spots. "Clean up in aisle five! Clean up in aisle five!" I say, pretending I'm in Walmart or something and overhearing the summons to maintenance over the PA.

You're losing it, dude!

I follow the trail until it reaches the far end of the warehouse near the fire exit. Nothing else. I wonder if the trail leads outside, but I don't open the fire door because I don't want to set off the fire alarm. I hear the door on the other end of the warehouse open, and there's the rush of feet and panicked voices. I turn to go back, and that's when I come face-to-face with Peter's head happily sitting on top of a box right at eye level. The mouth is agape in terror, and I notice the dude needs a dentist. The eyes are all bugged out, and there's a big fat fly sitting on one of them just looking up at me. Most of the scalp is missing, exposing red meat and a big hole, like the brains have been all sucked out with an oversize milkshake straw. A loud crack of thunder sounds, punctuating the macabre moment.

"Whoa, man!" I whisper. Then I shout to the oncoming stampede of freaked-out employees, "Yo, dudes! I found the head!"

10

GHOST

The present, downtown Montreal, early Wednesday morning

The police have finished taking our statements, and the Q & A sessions end with warnings about not leaving town. Brouchard seems devastated about Peter's murder, but I get the impression he's more annoyed that the warehouse is now a crime scene and he can't ship product until the scene is cleared. The entire night shift is just standing outside the building for a few minutes, talking quietly among ourselves while detectives, uniformed cops, crime-scene investigators, and the ME do their thing, giving us a wide berth now that we've answered all the questions of the night and claim to know nothing about a motive for Peter's untimely demise. I notice the sky has cleared. There are even a few stars. Things may be looking up.

"Long night," I say to Sue, who's standing next to me. She hasn't said much throughout this ordeal.

She looks up at me and says, "You can say that again."

"Been a long night."

"Oh, shut up," she says, but she laughs just a little. "You're a real character, you know that?"

"So I've been told," I say.

People are starting go. Tina and Chandi head to their car. I overhear them saying how terrible it is. "I'm going to give notice," Tina says. "You just wait."

"No, you're not," Chandi says. "We both need the money. And besides, who else is gonna hire chicks like us? Come on, let's jet!"

My investigative antennas perk up at something Chandi has said. *Who else is going to hire chicks like us?* Mannie was guilty of murder. *What is Peter's story? What is the story behind Tina and Chandi? What is the story behind all the rest of Brouchard's employees?* I decide it might be interesting to find out. It occurs to me that an employer who hires people with troubled pasts can hold it over them, keeping them in line and making them almost like indentured servants. *Is this how Brouchard has prospered?* Reducing turnover and keeping wages artificially low in a labor force can go a long way toward boosting the bottom line.

Tina and Chandi get in their car and drive off. Jean Claude has already gone. Jacques, Martin, and several others all say goodnight to Sue and me and head to their cars. We're alone, and yet we're not alone, what with all the cops scooting around.

I wave to my colleagues. I turn back to Sue and say, "I'm pretty wired. How about you?"

Sue sighs. "Yeah, wired to the max, if you want to know. Lord, I don't know what this world is comin' to."

"It's goin' to hell in a handbasket, if you ask me, but then nobody ever does," I say. "Listen, let me buy you a drink. It'll settle you down, and we got the day off tomorrow—uh, today—so we don't have to worry about that."

"What a way to get some down time." She hesitates, giving me a searching look. Her eyes look sad, even in the orange security lights that make them hard to see. "Well, I don't see why not," she says, straightening her blonde curls.

"Come on," I say. "Follow me in your car. I know a nice after-hours bar that's still serving food."

"Okay, but don't lose me," she says.

"I wouldn't think of it!" I say, noticing the slightest hint of a smile crossing her face. I like the smile. I think I like her, but who can tell, given all the emotional electricity flowing on this particular night.

I walk her to her car, a black BMW M3 GTS with a 4.4-liter V8 engine—a real sporty ride, and expensive.

"Man, I gotta work in HR! Sweet car, Sue!" I say, and I mean it. I actually find myself fighting off pangs of envy. I'm also wondering how she can afford a Beamer.

Sue laughs. "Glad you like it."

I give her directions to the bar in case we really do get separated in late-night downtown traffic, and I write my cell number down for her, just in case.

"You're such a gentleman, Michael."

"I aim to please."

We both cruise on out of the parking lot, and in a few minutes we're on the country roads outside the city. It's dark. Sue's high beams behind me are the only lights around. My window's open, and fresh clean air wafts in, tousling my hair. The passage of the storm has washed everything off, cleansing the cloying humidity away. Good old Canadian air from up north has blessed us with a visit. It's welcome. I feel a need for purity, for something that's untainted with evil, which I sense around me in a big way. I ride in silence without the radio, thinking about what has happened to Mannie and now to Peter. I'm thinking about the devil creature too. I'm more convinced than ever that I'm not having some kind of bad flashback from those days in California when I experimented with acid. I'm beginning to think the thing is real, and that it's behind the murders.

I catch something in the corner of my eye in the passenger seat. I glance over, and I'm shocked to see a woman with long, dark hair, who's dressed in white robes, seated next to me. She fades in and out, there one second and gone the next. I almost lose control of the car, swerving into the other lane before getting back on my side of the road.

"Save my son," the ghost woman says. "Please save my son! You are the only one who can!"

"Get out of here, ghost!" I shout. "Leave me alone! It's not bad enough that I have a devil creature prowling around. Now I have ghost ladies too?"

The apparition looks over at me, and I swear to Yahweh that she's crying. Tears stream down her beautiful face. She's got the saddest eyes I've ever seen in my life.

"My son is in danger," she says. "He has been in danger all his life, and now you are in danger too. You must stop the evil!"

Her voice is faint and garbled. It's like, man, it's like she's talking under water or something. "What?" I ask. "Can't hear you!"

"You heard me," the sexy ghost lady says.

"Not so much, man."

She gives me a stern look. "You must listen. I can only appear in this dimension to those of pure heart, and I cannot do it often. Even now I am straining to make myself known to you. I cannot appear to my son as I am now, only in his dreams. I can warn him, but I fear it will do no good. I fear his heart is already too corrupt. I fear the evil is too far entrenched within his soul, but it isn't in yours. You must ally yourself with him. As a man of pure heart, you must help him!"

"Who is your son?" I ask, humoring the sexy ghost lady.

"You know him," she says. "You've seen him in both his forms."

She reaches toward me, trying to touch my arm, but she disappears before she makes physical contact.

"Man, do I need a drink or what?" I say. I light a butt with trembling hands. I try to forget what I've just seen, but I can't. *I've seen him in both his forms?*

My cell rings. I answer it.

"Michael! What happened?"

It's Sue. She's tailgating me. The high beams practically blind me.

"You almost had an accident!" she says, stating the obvious.

I take a deep breath, then another drag on my cigarette. "I thought I saw something in the road. Didn't want to hit it," I lie.

"I didn't see anything."

"Guess I didn't either. Mind's playing tricks on me lately. Hey, you want to drop back or lower your beams? You're blinding me here!"

Sue's car drops back.

"Well, that was scary," she says. "I don't need any more scary tonight."

"Neither do I. Guess we shouldn't be talking on the phone while we're driving; no texting either. We'll be at the bar in a little while. I'm hanging up now. Got to concentrate on the road."

We hang up. I drive. *Did I really just see a ghost lady? And a pretty sad, sexy lady at that?*

A short time later, we enter Montreal proper, and I feel much better. The woods around Brouchard Inc. bother me for some reason, and I wonder if it's the spirits of dead Indians roaming around. I picture Peter's scalped head and consider that it's remotely possible that an Indian ghost did the deed, but after a few moments more of reflection I'm not buying it. Indians are cool, they don't do such things. I wonder about a lot of things, but I stop pondering after we arrive at the bar and I suck down a boilermaker. Sue orders a glass of red wine. We share a plate of cheeses and assorted crackers, along with bowls of French onion soup. It's too late at night for a heavy meal, and it's too early for breakfast, though if Sue could get grits and biscuits with gravy I bet she'd go for it. I watch her eat, and there's something sweet about her that makes me feel kinda tender inside. A real flash of the warm and fuzzy.

"I didn't realize I was even hungry," Sue says, slurping up some soup. "But I am. Maybe it's death that makes me want to eat. You know. Like after funerals everyone eats and drinks up a storm?"

"We sit Shiva," I say. "Jewish funerals are different from—what did you say you were? A Baptist? Yeah, our way is way different from that, I bet."

Sue eats her soup in silence. "I didn't know you were Jewish. You don't strike me as being Jewish."

"And how would a Jew strike you, Sue?"

"Oh, I don't know. Sometimes you can just tell."

I'm a little offended by that, but I've heard it before. I even suppose it's true in some cases, so I cut her some slack and let it go.

"I think there's a lot more in common between religions than what's different, is all," she continues. "I think we all believe in God, and that's there's only one God. Don't you?"

"Yeah, I believe in one God. We call Him Yahweh. I've looked to Yahweh a lot, and I still do."

She raises an eyebrow. "I look to Jesus."

"Doesn't surprise me. You're a Baptist."

"Guess so." She spears a piece of cheese with a toothpick and pops the cheese into her mouth. She sighs and leans back in her chair, looks me over as if for the first time. "I'm glad you're working for us, Michael. At a time like this we need the insights of an outsider."

Now it's me who raises an eyebrow. "What do you mean by 'outsider'?"

She coughs and straightens her hair, a habit I notice that comes out when she's nervous or upset.

"Oh, nothing. Just a figure of speech. You see, most of us have worked for Paul—uh, Mr. Brouchard—for years. Turnover is low, which is why HR is only one of my duties. We see ourselves as a kind of family. You know what I mean?"

I lift a spoonful of soup and swallow the liquid. It warms my throat. The melted cheese is excellent. I take another long slug of beer. I'm feeling better. Much better. Sue is enchanting me, and she's also intriguing me. I decide to poke around. "Mannie told me he had a past he was running from. Did you know about that?"

Sue gives me an appraising look and says, "Yes, I know his country of origin is, uh, *was* a little shaky. He may even have been here illegally, but—"

"And that didn't bother you or Mr. Brouchard?" I ask, interrupting her.

"No," she says. "No, not as long as Mannie did a good job and kept his nose clean with us. As long as he did that, he was welcome to join the family. Unlike lots of families, like mine, for example, the Brouchard family is accepting of people. We're tolerant of people and their faults. Jesus is all about forgiveness, you know."

Sue's sweetness is giving way to something just a tad creepy, as if she's drunk the Kool-Aid or something. Maybe she has. I'm disappointed.

"Mr. Brouchard's message in his church and in his business is all about forgiving sins and turning the other cheek. He's all about second chances, even if it means taking risks or even losing money. He's been through so much, you know. After Sarah's death, well, he seemed just lost, but he's found his way again in the Lord. We all do. We all get lost and then find our way. Don't you think so, Michael? Don't Jews believe the same thing?"

Sue is on a hell of a roll. I almost don't want to answer her, to see what she'll say next, but I do answer. I assure her Jews believe in redemption just as Christians do.

"Good," she says, and she shoots me a radiant smile. "I thought so."

"And did Peter have a past too?" I ask.

"Why, we all have pasts, Michael. Everybody does."

"A troubled past."

"Well, yes," she says after pausing a moment, as though she is buying time to figure out whether she wants to answer or not. "He did some time. But he's a good worker, a real gentleman, a real—

Her voice trails off. She looks down, dabs her full lips with the corner of her paper napkin, and begins to cry softly.

"Did time for what?"

"Armed robbery." Sniffle. Another sniffle.

"Oh."

Sue blows her nose in her napkin. It's a loud, wet, squishy snot blow.

"Hey, hey, it's okay, Sue," I say, reaching out and putting my hand over hers. "It's been tough, what with Mannie and Peter both dying the way they did. Real tough."

"Yes, it is." She looks over at me. "Something tells me we're not out of the woods yet either. I sense an evil presence, as if it's trying to get Paul. As if, well, as if it's after all of us."

I remain silent, hoping she'll keep talking, but she doesn't. Do I tell her I feel the same thing? Do I tell her I've seen a devil creature? I decide to keep my mouth shut. Based on what I've just heard, any mention of a devil creature will wig her out big time! She's given me more insights into Brouchard and his company and the people he hires. Then I begin to wonder why I was hired. I have secrets too. Only Laurent knows about those, and I'm sure he hasn't been talking out of school.

"Uh, it's like—well, it's like normal to feel that way, given what's happened," I say lamely.

She nods and takes another sip of her wine, draining the glass.

I polish off my beer.

"I think I should go," she says. "I'm tired. It was nice, you asking me to come out with you. I think I can sleep now. Hope so, anyway."

I agree, and we both go after I pay the check. Out on the sidewalk we are almost entirely alone. The streets are quiet. The night sky is that deep black that only comes just before dawn. Soon it will be light out. I yawn, not bothering to hide it.

"I could use some shut-eye," I say as I walk Sue to her car.

"Me too," she says.

We stop in front of her Beamer.

"Thanks, Michael," she says. She stands on her tiptoes and gives me a quick peck on the lips. Not the cheek. The lips. I find that promising.

Watch out, dude! I warn myself. *This chick could be bad news!*

"Get some sleep, Sue. Everything'll look better in the morning."

"No, I'm afraid it won't, but thanks for sayin' so anyways. 'Night," she says, and she gets in her car and fires up the engine.

I stand with my hands on my hips and watch her go, the car fading into the shadows.

11

BLOOD CHILDREN

The present, Montreal, Brouchard residence, Wednesday morning

Paul Brouchard sits in his living room with a highball glass of Glenlivet 18 single-malt Scotch whisky cradled in his right hand. His hand is trembling, and even the soothing warmth of the eighteen-year-old nectar served neat doesn't calm his shot nerves in these intense predawn hours. Hoping for better results, he takes another sip, and then a bigger one after that, emptying half the glass. He sighs and looks around at the luxurious and yet rustic décor of the home. Sarah's tastes guided all, even if the leanings were a little over the top for a preacher.

"Sarah, darling! Let's not forget who I am," he'd said as they were selecting furniture, rugs, paintings, appliances, landscaping, and all the rest of the things that went into an upscale home. "I don't want my flock to get the wrong idea about me."

"Nonsense, Paul! Everyone knows you've built a thriving manufacturing business with the help of the good Lord. Everyone knows that the business came before you became a preacher. Everyone knows you've always given to charity and supported good causes around the city. Let the bleating little sheep talk! Ha! Bah! I don't care, and neither should you!"

Sarah proceeded to buy everything she wanted. She loved playing house and spending his money, and he loved watching her do it. Everything stayed the same after Stanley and Lizzie's adoptions were finalized. If anything, Sarah had become even more lavish, spoiling both children with the latest electronic games, space camp during the summer, and long vacations to Orlando to see Mickey Mouse strut his stuff in Florida.

Brouchard stares at the Scotch in a crystal decanter on the mahogany glass-topped coffee table. It's within easy reach, which comforts him, at least a little. He stares at the paintings hung on the walls, subdued Impressionist landscapes, and then he looks over at the stuffed elk head mounted above the fireplace. It was a gift from Sarah's uncle, who still loves to hunt all over the world. Brouchard shakes his head and laughs. "Money can't buy you everything," he says. "Only the Lord Jesus can bring you real peace. I think you forgot that, Sarah. I think I let you forget."

Beneath Brouchard's feet—warm and snug in worn-out fluffy slippers his wife gave him shortly before her death—is a large genuine Oriental carpet that cost the equivalent of half a year's salary for his senior employees. The blond oak hardwood floors glisten around its perimeter. The furnishings are all exotic wood and soft leather with brass ornamentation. The curtains are done in red velvet. They are a bit heavy to suit his tastes, but Sarah wanted a slightly Victorian country feel for the house, and so he kept protests to a minimum.

Now he is alone without the only woman he ever loved, and he misses her. Life has never been the same since she inexplicably swerved off the road into a ravine, where the gas tank exploded, engulfing the car in flames. Witnesses said it was as if she were trying to avoid hitting something, but there was no hard of evidence of anything like that happening. She'd been burned so badly the medical examiner had needed dental records to make a positive ID.

For years now Brouchard had been battling images of her burning alive—screaming and praying to God to help her, to spare her—and for years he'd been battling the anger within him about the apparent injustice and random nature of God's will. Obviously, there had been a closed coffin at Sarah's funeral. The last time he ever saw his wife's brilliant smile, her deep-blue eyes, or her curly shoulder-length brown hair was on the morning he rushed to work without even kissing her goodbye. Pictures of her remind him of what he has lost, but in his mind's eye his visual recollections of her have already faded.

Since the accident, Brouchard has tried very hard to be a good father to Stanley and Lizzie, a good preacher to his congregation, and a good boss to everyone who works at Brouchard Inc., but as he sits contemplating all the darkness and grief that has accompanied him throughout his life, he can't help but feel bitter and angry. A fly buzzes around his head, landing on his thinning dark hair. He bats the fly away. It comes back. It seems intent upon stirring him from his thoughts, and for a moment he's grateful to the fly. He swats at it again as it buzzes past his left ear. He misses and hits himself instead. The fly veers away and lands on a nearby lamp.

"Get out of here, fly!" Brouchard says. "I'll get the bug spray out if you don't leave me alone!"

The fly seems to hear him. It disappears as if by magic. Brouchard doesn't know where the fly has gone, and he doesn't really care. "Just stay away from me!" he says. He takes another drink of Scotch. "You hear me? Just stay away! I've got enough things bugging me right now."

Brouchard drains his glass and then refills it. He's feeling a little drunk. He's glad about that. He needs to feel a little drunk. A murder right in his warehouse, and not just any murder. A gruesome, horrible head-chopping murder that he's certain will grab headlines in all the big daily newspapers—just like the headlines that splashed across the front pages in April 1986 when his parents were killed and set on fire by an unknown assailant. Except he has an idea of who, or what, had done it. He is sure the devil creature in his dreams was somehow responsible. He is sure the creature was more than a simple figment of his subconscious mind, and yet, after all these years, he'd never dreamed of the creature again.

Yes, the papers will dig up all the old dirt on the Brouchards. The terrible murders of my adoptive parents and Sarah's agonizing death in the fiery car accident. If Mannie's murder isn't enough to get the media's juices going on my family's past, then Peter's murder definitely will be, he thinks.

"Damned vultures!" he says, swirling the Scotch around in his nearly full glass. "You'll drive me into my grave. Damned reporters with all their questions, all their digging, all their gloating, and all their exploitation of the misery of others."

Close to utter despair, Brouchard empties and fills his glass several more times, until his head throbs and he starts seeing trails in the corners of his eyes, bright streaks that swirl and twirl. He feels dizzy and a little nauseous.

"Time for bed," he mumbles as he gets up from the loveseat and staggers upstairs. He wobbles over to Stanley's bedroom and pokes his head inside. He can make out the sleeping young man in his bed by the overhead light in the hallway. Satisfied, he does the same with his daughter before meandering toward the master suite, careful not to bump into the walls or to fall down the stairs. Once he reaches the refuge of the master suite, he drops into bed, dead tired. He's too tired to think and too tired to stay awake a moment longer.

The nightmares begin almost immediately. There's a flash of bright light and a dizzying surge upward, as if he's on an elevator about to launch out of the stratosphere, and his stomach drops. He's screaming and thrashing. He feels like an insect caught in a spider's web. He opens his eyes wide and sees the familiar jungle setting, only this time there's a long dirt road at his feet. Dense vegetation hems in the road, and a thick canopy of branches and leaves darkens the path even though it's daytime.

Before him is a young woman dressed in white robes. She has long, dark hair and sad eyes. He has never seen her in his dreams or nightmares, but he recognizes the bearded man with the eye patch as the one who kisses snakes. The young woman kneels in front of Snake Kisser. Brouchard watches, as if he is invisible, and perhaps he is.

"Father," the woman says, "you have done enough! I will not permit your evil to live on in my grandchildren! I will not! I will fight you! I will chase you to the ends of the earth, the ends of the stars! I will chase you into the never-ending blackness where no starlight falls!"

Snake Kisser laughs hysterically. "You dared to defy me once! You dare to defy me again? You will now pay double for your sins!"

Brouchard opens his mouth to scream as the bearded man draws a long silver dagger from a sheath he wears on a sash across his midriff. The blade is bright against Snake Kisser's black robes, shining as if it's in the direct sun instead of in the shadows. It is not supposed to shine in such dim ambient light, but it does anyway. "You will submit to me now or pay the price forever!" the bearded man shouts. "You and all you love! You and all you love forever! Do you hear me?"

"No!" Brouchard yells. He somehow knows the woman, but he can't figure out who she is or where he's seen her. He only knows he must protect her from the snake man he's seen so many times in his nightmares—the snake kisser under the crimson clouds and that eerie orange crescent moon. He struggles, but the invisible spiderweb holds him tight. The more he struggles, the less he is able to move. "No, run! Run away from him!"

The woman in white robes gets to her feet and takes several steps back.

"You are too late," the bearded snake kisser shouts at her. "You are too late to stop me and my kind! You are too late for the world! You are too late for your son and grandchildren!"

Brouchard writhes and kicks his legs. He punches the air and shouts. He can't move, and suddenly he sees that he really is in a spiderweb and that its maker, a great big black spider, is inching toward him, its deep-yellow eyes cold and lifeless. He can see the spider's mouth salivating and moving up and down in anticipation of a Happy Meal. "Oh God! Save me! Save the woman in white! Oh Jesus!"

"You do not have power over me, Father!" the woman says, her voice strong and still defiant. "You only have power over the weak! Be gone! I rebuke you in Allah's name!"

The bearded snake kisser looks shocked and really pissed. But he doesn't move to attack her with the dagger. Instead, there is a mighty clap of thunder, and he vanishes in a split second.

"Get me outta here!" Brouchard screams. "Spider! Big hairy, hungry spider at twelve o'clock high! *Eek! Yikes! Holy cow! Get me outta here!*"

The woman in white approaches, looks at the spider, and holds her hands out as if she is a cop stopping traffic. The spider looks very disappointed, but it stops. "Come no closer!" she commands. "Come closer and you die!"

The spider bends its legs and claps its spit-dripping jaws a few times. It glares at the woman in white robes, and then it, too, disappears. There is now only Brouchard stuck in the web and the woman in white robes amidst the dense jungle. It is getting darker by the moment. Thunder rolls in the distance.

The woman draws a dagger of her own and begins to slash the spiderweb, cutting him down. He falls heavily and the wind is knocked from his lungs. Coughing, he struggles to his feet as he pulls the gauzy sticky threads away from his business suit. He looks down and sees that his dress shoes are ruined.

"Son of a bitch," he says. "There's spidey spit on my shoes! I just bought these!"

The woman in white robes puts both hands on his shoulders and says, "Forget about your shoes! My son! Oh, my dear, sweet son!"

Brouchard is stunned. He stares deeply into the woman's eyes. There is definitely something familiar about them. "Mother?"

"There is not much time, my son! Listen, and listen well!"

"But—"

"No time!" the woman screams, and Brouchard reels backward. The woman points a finger at him. "You have been cursed. You carry the evil of your grandfather and the great dark one, and that has guided and shaped your life without you even knowing it! He is inside you, and you must rebuke him just as you saw me do!"

"B-b-but, but—"

"*Silence!*" Now her voice thunders. Lightning slashes the sky, shining through gaps in the jungle canopy. The sun vanishes behind banks of black clouds. "The evil in you already rebels!"

"I am not evil!" Brouchard manages to shout. "I'm a man of God!"

"You are both! You just do not know it! You must look to your God, to your Jesus! You must call upon the power of your Lord to banish the evil! You must keep your children free of it, or your grandfather will take them too! Look for an ally, my son! One is close! Very close!"

"My grandfather is—"

"You will be silent! No time! No time to—"

"Can't I get a word in edgewise around here? I mean, come on!"

A dark look crosses the woman's face. A gust of wind billows out her white robes. She screams above the gale that suddenly has begun to blow, bending the trees and nearly knocking Brouchard down.

"You may be a lost cause, my son! But I call upon you to stop the curse. Stop the curse! If it passes to your children, their evil will be ten times as powerful as yours! You must not let that happen! You must rebuke the evil! Most important, you must keep the blood of your veins away from the mouths of the innocent!"

A tremendous blast of wind hurls Brouchard to the ground and rolls him hard into an enormous tree. The woman in white disappears, and just above him the giant spider reappears and begins to amble slowly down the trunk of the tree, licking its chops.

"No! No! Lord, protect me!" Brouchard yells, backing away from the tree with his butt still on the ground as he pushes backward with his feet and hands.

The spider is almost upon him, its yellow eyes glinting with hunger. The black creature seems almost to be grinning.

"Oh God! Oh no, no—!"

Brouchard lurches awake in his bed, eyes wide open. His breathing is labored, his heart is pumping fast, and he's soaked in sweat. He knows he's had a terrific nightmare. He senses that it's the worst one yet, but his memory of it is fading fast.

"Think! Remember! You must remember!" he mutters as he sits up, swings his legs over the edge of the bed, and puts on his fluffy slippers.

I know this one is important! I know it! Remember, you son of a bitch! You must remember!

The last tendrils of the dream run like tiny silver strands across his mind. There are images, but they are fading fast. The last thing he remembers is the face of a beautiful woman. *She's trying to tell me something! What? What are you trying to tell me?* And then she's gone and there's a really spooky spider coming at him. Then everything goes blank in his mind.

"Damn it!"

Brouchard can remember nothing. He stands up. His knees feel weak. His head hurts more now than it did before. He loudly inhales and exhales, and then he walks to the picture window overlooking his vast property. Dawn has arrived. Shadows begin to retreat. The sky is already a deep blue. He makes his way downstairs to the kitchen and begins to prepare breakfast for his kids, deciding that an omelet would be a nice change from cold cereal. There's no rush. The factory is closed.

After several trips to the refrigerator, he's got mushrooms, green peppers, onions, Swiss cheese, eggs, butter, and grape jelly for toast out on the granite countertop. He starts chopping, his mind lost in the confusion that has shaken his very soul. That impending sense of doom is heavy on his shoulders. Its weight presses down, making it almost hard to breathe. Distracted, he slices open his middle finger with the paring knife. Blood squirts out onto the cutting board.

"Damn it!" he says. "Clumsy fool!"

He runs water over the wound, wipes up the cutting board, and gets a Band-Aid out of the medicine cabinet in the downstairs half-bath to cover the cut. He sees the cut is deep, but he doesn't think he'll need stitches. Back in the kitchen, he continues preparing the meal. He sees he's missed a couple drops of blood, and he dabs them up with a paper towel. Then he gets the veggies into a hot frying pan. They sizzle and fill the kitchen with a pleasant homey fragrance, and he thinks of mornings like this when Sarah was still a part of his life. Part of Stanley and Lizzie's lives.

"Dad?"

Brouchard turns at the sound of Stanley's voice and gives his son a big smile. "Morning, Stanley! Sleep well?"

Stanley stretches his arms over his head as he stands on his toes to loosen up his leg muscles. "Yeah, okay, I guess. What're you doin'?"

"Making breakfast."

Before Stanley can say another word, Brouchard hears the running footsteps of his daughter as she rushes down the stairs. A second later she's in the kitchen, standing next to her brother.

"Mmm! Yum! What smells so yummy?" she asks, rushing over and hugging Brouchard's leg.

He reaches down and tousles her hair. He looks down at her and she looks up at him. "A nice omelet for three!" he says.

"I don't feel like an omelet," Stanley says, going to the refrigerator and taking a half-gallon of milk out. He opens the carton and starts drinking.

"Stanley, get a glass, okay?" Brouchard says. He stirs the vegetables in the frying pan.

"I want bacon too!" Lizzie says.

"Sorry, sweetie, we're out of bacon."

"Aw."

"Get a glass, Stanley!" Brouchard says, forcing himself to sound stern.

Stanley says nothing, but he fetches a glass from one of the cabinets and pours some milk into the glass. He sits down at the table with his sister. Lizzie holds her fork, prongs up, and hits the table with the butt end.

"We want bacon! We want bacon!" she says, and then she giggles when Brouchard throws a little piece of pepper at her. She picks up the pepper and eats it.

"Food fight!" Stanley yells, and he dashes to the cutting board. He grabs a piece of pepper, pops it into his mouth, and then grabs another one and pelts Brouchard with it.

Looking down at the middle finger of his right hand, Brouchard sees that the blood has soaked through the pad of the Band-Aid. Rivulets of bright-red blood run down his hand and wrist.

Maybe I do need stitches, he thinks.

"What happened to your finger, Dad?" Stanley asks.

"Oh, it's nothing," he says, but that impending sense of doom he's felt for a long time, and even more intensely over the past forty-eight hours, feels more acute than ever. Uneasy, he wraps the finger in a damp paper towel. "Hold on while I go take care of this finger," he says. "Then we'll have a nice breakfast before I get you guys to school."

Sabbah had remained in Brouchard's house, sitting on the curtain rod in the master suite just watching the cursed one sleep. Now Sabbah is in the kitchen, hiding on top of a cabinet. He takes great delight in what he sees, the blood from Brouchard's cut getting into the food the innocents are eating at this very moment!

Ah, it is as I thought, Sabbah thinks. *It is as I've always known and hoped! I have my new recruits! I have my new instruments of death, more powerful even than the adoptive father, Brouchard!*

His mission done, Sabbah waits near the front door. When Brouchard opens the door to usher the kids to the car, Sabbah flies out. The children will sicken fast, and they will cry and gnash their teeth in pain. But then they will emerge from the process.

Yes, Sabbah thinks. *Yes, they'll emerge quite nicely indeed!*

12

STORIED PASTS

The present, outside Montreal, Brouchard Inc., Wednesday afternoon

I wake up late after the night from hell at Brouchard Inc., which happened to end okay with my entertaining Sexy Sue at the twenty-four-hour bar. The insights she shared were helpful as well, and I think about the whole burrito as I take a shower. I know a couple of things for sure. Brouchard's not all that he seems. His second-chance thing with the employees sounds great on paper, but it somehow doesn't sit well with me. He gives jobs to apparently rehabilitated criminals, which is fine, but why is everyone so secretive about it? And why have two employees guilty of past crimes ended up as deadsters?

After washing my hair, I lather up my face and look up at the showerhead. The steaming water jets pelt my skin and beat on my closed eyelids. It feels great.

I recall from my fake rat hunt in Brouchard's office that both Mannie's and Peter's names were on the list written on those yellow pieces of legal paper. I suspect Brouchard removed the list from his locked desk drawer as soon as I left his office, but on the off-chance he didn't, I decide to head on over to the factory to take another look when the coast is clear. Don't know when that'll be either. Cops are likely to still be crawling all over the place, but then again, maybe not. As gross as the crime scene was, it was pretty straightforward. Besides, Brouchard would push hard to get the scene cleared so he could resume production and shipping.

Anyway, if I can get my hands on that list, I figure I can cross-reference all the names with the names of individuals now on holiday six feet under. A pattern might emerge, and I might be able to pinpoint who's next—like me. The idea I could be a member of the hit parade puckers my ass, I can tell you that! Maybe I can get to a motive for the murders as well. I still can't put my finger on the devil creature, and the ghost lady in white has me all weirded out. It all just seems so surreal.

All soaped up and rinsed, I turn the shower off, get out of the stall, and start drying myself off. I rub my skin hard to get the blood flowing while looking in the mirror and flexing my muscles. It works, a little. My landline rings. I wrap the damp towel around my waist and cruise to the phone.

"Hello?"

"Michael? Laurent. I just heard it on the news! You got another stiff over at Brouchard Inc."

"I don't have one. A stiff, I mean. Brouchard's got one, big time! Me and the night super found the DB, and get this! The dude was missing his fuckin' head, man! His whole head!"

Silence for a long moment. "Yeah, I know. That little detail has the newshounds baying at the moon!"

"Yeah, man, I'm tellin' you! It was gnarly. Gross as crap with all these little white things sticking—"

"Spare me the details, Michael."

"Oh. Yeah. Sure . . . . So what's up, boss?"

"I'm calling to see if you want to be reassigned. I won't blame you if you do."

I answer without hesitation. "No, I'm on it."

"Are you sure? Working for Paul Brouchard is starting to look like a pretty unhealthy proposition."

"Yeah, I'm sure. Hey, look at it as practice for when I get my PI creds!"

Laurent laughs.

"It's all pretty freaky, though," I say. I'm starting to get cold standing by the phone dressed only in a towel. My dick is burrowing into full retraction mode.

"Yeah, it is freaky," Laurent says.

"I found out the latest victim also had an unsavory past. Like Mannie."

"They haven't released the guy's name yet," Laurent says. "Who's the latest vic?"

"The dude's name was Peter Galipo. Not a bad guy. Just a little on the sleazy side, to tell the truth. He's got a record. Rap sheet includes armed robbery. So that makes two employees with funky resumes."

"How'd you find that out?"

"I wormed it out of the cute HR chick over there. From what she says, everybody's got secrets or yesterdays they don't want to remember. She made Brouchard out to be some kind of saint or some such shit. Called the employees *family*. I don't believe a word of it, though. There's more going on than someone offing reformed crooks."

"Care to elaborate?" Laurent sounds very curious now. Like me, he's a born snooper. I toy with the idea of filling him in on the supernatural stuff that seems to permeate the events surrounding the murders, but I decide it's not in my best interests to give the boss the idea that I've only got one shoe laced and the other one three sheets to the wind.

"Not now, man," I say. "Let me dig around a little more."

"You need me to look into anyone else?"

"Yeah, you could find out if the HR chick lied about Peter. Maybe he was into more than just robbing people at gunpoint or with a machete or whatever."

"Will do," Laurent says. "And Michael. Be careful, will you? I don't want to lose my rising star detective to some psycho serial killer with a grudge against ex-cons."

"You got it, boss!"

Laurent says goodbye and we hang up. I finish drying off, get dressed, and grab a quick bite at the corner café. My cell rings while I'm eating.

"Hello?"

"Michael?"

"Oh, hi, Sue! Long time no see," I say while chomping my buttered croissant.

"Hi. I got a lot of calls to make, so I got to make this fast," she says, getting right to the point.

"Okay."

"The police have cleared the crime scene, and—"

"That was fast!" I say, but I'm also thinking about my planned recon mission. I'm wondering whether this is going to mess it up or actually help.

"Yeah," Sue says, "I guess it is. Regular work schedules begin starting tomorrow."

"No rest for the weary," I say.

"Yeah, no rest for the weary," she says. "Hey, Michael?"

"Yeah?"

"Thanks for last night, uh, I mean earlier this morning. You were a real gentleman, and I'm grateful."

"Don't give it a second thought, Sue. I enjoyed your company too!"

"Okay, then. Well, I gotta go."

We say our goodbyes. I finish my croissant, which is now cold. I finish my coffee, pay up, and head out to my car. *Am I "good to go"?* I wonder. I figure that now is as good a time as any for the recon I want to do. I drive out to the factory. It's midafternoon by the time I get close. On the way, I've been trying to decide just how I want to handle my next move. Chances are the cops aren't all gone. They're probably staking the place out. They're no doubt hoping that the killer, or killers, might return to the scene of the crime. It's not as silly as it sounds. Criminals actually do that. I don't want to take the risk of being stopped by the cops. On the other hand, the damned place is out in the middle of nowhere. You can't approach it without being seen. There's a vast lawn around the facility, and woods hem it in on all sides. The access road is the only way in or out.

I finally just say the hell with it and drive around the building, checking things out. No cars parked in obvious places. I figure cop cars could be parked out of sight inside the building in the loading area, but I won't be able to tell from out here. Satisfied to a point, I drive right on up to the building and park near the front entrance.

I let myself in, disarm and rearm the alarm system, and make a beeline right for Brouchard's office. I'm not surprised to discover my master key doesn't work anymore, but I've brought my lock-pick kit. I'm inside in less than two minutes. I half expect to see Mr. Devil Creature seated behind Brouchard's desk, but there's nobody or nothing untoward inside the office as I get on all fours and crawl along the carpet protector, feeling for the key.

No key.

I come out from under the desk and try all the drawers. Every single one is locked. I pick the locks and find nothing unusual. In fact, the Canadian Club, rubbers, reefer, and the oversize Manila envelope have all been removed from the bottom drawer. I figure the list and the clips could be anywhere, even in the shredder, so I don't waste any more time searching the office. Trying not to be too pissed off about going on a wild goose chase, I let myself out, making sure the door is locked behind me, and I walk quickly toward the site of the crime scene figuring I might discover something. Just what, I'm not sure. I'm working more on autopilot at this point. I'm halfway there when I hear footsteps behind me.

"RCMP! Freeze!"

Oh shit!

"Hands behind your head!"

I comply and start to turn around. "Hey, look guys, I—"

"Shut up! Stay where you are! Don't move!"

I hear footsteps close behind me and the sound of one pistol getting holstered. Simultaneously I feel the tight grip of a big dude on both my wrists as my arms are pulled behind my back. I feel the cold steel of the handcuffs and hear them lock closed. The big dude pushes them tight. Tight enough to hurt like hell.

"I'm tellin' you—"

I'm whipped around to face the wall. Hands go over me in a thorough frisk, and they find the lock-pick kit.

Not good!

They also find my company ID.

Good!

"Michael Abraham," one of the officers says, spinning me around to face him. "You mind telling us what you're doing here?"

The other guy holsters his gun.

"I work here, dude! What are you doing here?"

I hate tangling with cops, and I especially hate tangling with Royal Canadian Mounted Police, Canada's version of the American FBI. It just doesn't make my day, you know? The dude strong-arming me looks like a linebacker for the New York Giants. He's got at least two inches on me, which makes him at least six foot two. He's clean-shaven and has a military-style haircut. His partner is also a heavy. I peg both dudes as ex-military, probably from the Canadian Special Forces Operations Command, real badass mothers you just don't want to mess with.

Big Dude waves the lock-pick kit under my nose. "So your ID says." He ignores my lame query and gets on with his line of questioning. "So, if you're with company security, why do you have this on you, eh?"

"Uh, well, uh . . ."

"Well, Mr. Abraham?"

Big Dude's partner just stands there glaring at me.

I think fast. I've been seeing a chick at the university, a knockout grad student in biology, of all things, and I figure she'll back me up in a pinch. I go for it. "I helped my girlfriend get back into her apartment last night, or, well, very early this morning. She got locked out and called me for help. I went over there and helped her out, man! Forgot the kit was still in my pocket."

"These are illegal, you know, except for a licensed locksmith. You a locksmith, Mr. Abraham?" Other Big Dude asks.

"No, uh, but in my business it pays to be able to open locks."

Big Dude wasn't buying my story. Other Big Dude looked skeptical too.

"What's her name?" Big Dude asks. "Your damsel in distress."

"Lauren Belcourt."

"Phone?"

I give him Lauren's number, praying that my luck holds and she's not there.

He calls.

Oh no! She's there! Big Dude's talking. Now he's listening. Oh shit!

"Uh-huh. Yes, that's right. What time was that?"

The conversation ends a little while later.

"Well, your story checks out on the lock-pick kit," Big Dude says.

"Now tell us what you're doing here," Other Big Dude says. "The company's still closed."

"I'm in charge of security. I felt real bad about what happened to Peter Galipo, so I figured I'd come in to see if there was some kind of security breach, you know? It's just terrible that a killer could get in here like that."

Big Dude hands me back my lock-pick kit. "We'll forget we saw you with that," he says. "Anything you can tell us about the case?"

Suddenly we're pals, and that's just fine with me. I tell them what I know, that I think the same guy killed Mannie, that someone is targeting the employees, and that the employees have storied pasts. Of course, I say nothing about the devil creature.

"It's still unclear why no one heard the murder taking place," Other Big Dude says. "It wasn't a body dump. The killing occurred right where the body was found. So it seems unlikely that nobody heard a thing. And there was a prayer meeting in progress. Nobody missed Galipo, when they'd seen him on his shift earlier? Things just don't add up. Makes us think this is an inside job, which makes you a suspect, Mr. Abraham."

"Yeah, me and everyone else who was working at the time."

"True," Big Dude says. "Quite true. But you see why we have questions."

"Of course," I say. "Look, I'd like to keep looking around, Is that okay? Maybe another set of eyes might help."

Big Dude nods. "We've been over this place with a fine-toothed comb, but go ahead. Knock yourself out. We'll keep an eye on you while you do."

"Fine," I say. "And I shouldn't be a suspect."

"You show up all by your lonesome when you think nobody's around, and it could look to us like you were trying to find evidence you somehow left behind or hid." Big Dude smiles, but his smile is unfriendly.

"You here for the reappearing killer then?"

"Actually, we're here to offer extra security. Our orders came straight from Ottawa."

"Impressive!" I say.

"You might say Paul Brouchard is well connected," Other Big Dude says.

"Well, you guys want to tag along while I look around some more?"

"Don't mind if we do," both men say almost at once. "We'd hate for you to get lonely."

"Now, that'd be a crime," Other Big Dude says.

"Suit yourselves," I say.

13

DEVIL'S OWN

The present, outside Montreal, Brouchard Inc., Thursday, 9:00 to 10:35 p.m.

The employees of the night shift gather together with Sue, me, and Jean Claude, in the assembly area, to listen to what Paul Brouchard has to say. There's even a PA system set up around a makeshift stage. Folding chairs are arrayed in front of the stage. Tina, Chandi, Jacques, Martin, Pierre, Adrian, Francois, and a bunch of other employees I don't know but have seen around, congregate in their respective tribal cliques. They all look tired. Many have dark crescent moons under their lower eyelids. Many look very worried, even frightened.

As to the purpose of this little love fest, I figure Brouchard wants to tamp down any panic in the ranks and to assure everyone that it's safe to work in the building, even though the killer or killers are still at large. I'm wishing I had a handgun more than ever, but I can run pretty fast, so I conclude that my odds are excellent if it comes down to another dance with the devil creature. I glance over at Sue, who's standing next to me looking cute as a button.

"The boss make the day shift meet like this?" I ask.

Sue nods. "Paul—uh, Mr. Brouchard—just wants to make sure y'all aren't worried about anything else happening, is all. I think it's right smart, if you ask me. Corporations best communicate with the workers in a time of crisis, or they won't have any workers left to communicate with! You know what I mean, Michael?"

I lean over and whisper, "I see what you're saying."

"I'm especially proud of Mr. Brouchard in how he's handling this terrible mess," Sue goes on. "You know, his two kids got really sick yesterday. Is there anything else poor Paul—uh, Mr. Brouchard—must endure? The man's at the end of his rope, and yet here he is ready to give us a pep talk. Ready to lead us in prayer."

"What's wrong with his kids?" I ask, not really caring.

"They both got some really bad stomach virus or something. Dang near put the little babies in the ER."

"Humph," I say. "Sounds nasty."

"Yeah, real nasty, or so Mr. Brouchard told me this morning. He was up half the night with both of them. Came on real sudden, the virus did. Doctors thought it was food poisoning, but they've ruled that out. They don't really know what's going on, if you ask me," Sue says, her voice conspiratorial and just loud enough for me to hear over the low murmur of the restless crowd.

"Our boss seems to be having some very bad luck lately," I say.

Sue sucks in a big gulp of air, shakes her head as if she's just surfaced from a dive in a swimming pool, and exhales. "Oh yes! It's just terrible! Just terrible!"

I stop leaning down to hear Sue's conspiratorial patter, straighten up, and say, "Looks like the big boss is going to make his speech."

I glance down and see that Sue is smiling broadly. Her eyes gleam with anticipation. She's got Brouchard fixed in a penetrating and yet warm stare, a stare full of adoration. I scope out the others. Most now have similar looks. I wonder if there's something funky in the water around here. I check out the two officers from the Royal Canadian Mounted Police standing in the back, arms crossed, suit jackets bulging with the humps of their holstered semiautomatic pistols. Big Dude and Other Big Dude look stoic and bored out of their skulls. Don't blame 'em a bit either.

Brouchard taps the microphone two or three times and says, "Is this thing on?"

Some in the crowd laugh halfheartedly.

"My good people," Brouchard says in his deep preacher's voice, "we are gathered here tonight to pay our respects for our two fallen family members. What has happened is a tragedy, a gross injustice, a smear on the Brouchard company's good name. But such things happen in a wicked world. No matter how hard good tries to prevail, there is always evil standing in the wings to wipe out the effort. We can't let the deaths of Mannie and Peter stand in our way. We must be strong! We must have faith in the Lord!"

Brouchard's voice is rising. He's gesturing, pivoting, and pacing back and forth with the microphone in his right hand.

"The Lord Jesus watches over us all. He is the savior. He will guide and protect us as we go through this difficult time."

I study the crowd. For some odd reason, they seem transfixed by Brouchard. He's a good speaker, I'll give him that, but his words ring hollow to me. I believe God does guide and protect us all, but I have serious doubts that Brouchard really believes that. I sense something in him that just doesn't add up, doesn't sit right. I don't trust him. His smile hides something. Whenever I look into his eyes I feel the hairs on the back of my neck stand on end, and I don't know why.

Brouchard goes on for a while, assuring everyone that the police have the matter well in hand. He says the two officers are here to help me maintain proper security in case another event occurs. *Event.* That's the word he uses. I think it's a bit funny that he's never once used the word murder. Talk about trying to spin a disaster. He concludes his speech by leading everyone in prayer.

"Everyone take the hand of your neighbor," Brouchard says.

I take Sue's hand, and less enthusiastically I take Jean Claude's hand. He seems as uncomfortable as I am, and I can't help but smile. Silently, I say my own prayer to Yahweh, and I must say I feel comforted. I think of what the ghost lady said in the car, all that stuff about my being of pure heart and knowing her son, have seen him in both his forms. It strikes me that she might have been talking about the devil creature, but who is her son in the other form? Is it Brouchard? And do I really have a pure heart? I kinda doubt it.

"God bless you one and all," Brouchard says.

I immediately think of Tiny Tim in the Dickens story about Scrooge.

The meeting breaks up.

"Wasn't he just wonderful?" Sue says, looking up at me with eyes full of tears. "I feel so much better."

"He was his usual self," Jean Claude says noncommittally.

I shoot him a knowing look, and I swear he winks at me. *I may have misjudged this dude,* I think. "Yeah, he was pretty inspirational," I say. "Least the crowd seems to think so. I never knew a workplace where you got a dose of religion along with a scrawny paycheck."

Jean Claude actually laughs, and then his face goes serious. Sue frowns.

"Well, I guess I better make the rounds."

"I got paperwork to catch up on," Sue says. "Don't be surprised to see me in my office, Michael."

I nod.

"Okay, everybody, let's get a move on!" Jean Claude says as he strides over to Chandi, Tina, and Martin, who are talking among themselves. They scatter like pheasants flushed from the brush.

I stroll over to the Dudes and say hello. "Nice speech," I say.

"If you say so," Other Big Dude says.

"You guys hanging around here for a reason?"

"None that I can fathom. Orders from higher up. The brain trusts seem to think the perp will show himself, just waltz right in so we can apprehend him," Big Dude says. "Let's just say I have my doubts, eh?"

I laugh. "I know how that goes. Well, I'll be cruising around as usual, checking things out."

"You go do that," Other Big Dude says. "We'll do the same."

I give them both a mock salute.

"Go on, get the hell outta here," Big Dude says with a smile.

I comply.

The factory seems all quiet, all normal. I'm pleased, because I've had enough excitement for the time being. All I want is to put in my shift, go home, and hit the sack. I unlock the loading dock door and step out into the parking lot, alert for any suspicious movements in the looming shadows. The night air is cool and refreshing, and I linger awhile near the rear of the building. A gentle breeze swishes through the nearby pines.

Suddenly, I see a white ephemeral light in the woods. It moves slowly toward me, and then in a flash it's right next to me.

"Oh crap!"

The pretty ghost lady in white robes fades in and out. Her faint voice comes to me as if from a galaxy far, far away.

"I shouldn't have followed my heart. I have caused too much pain. I should've obeyed my father."

"Are you talking to me?" I ask, backing away from her. I whip out my Maglite and shine it at her. The beam goes right through her and lights up the trees. She doesn't seem to hear me, because she keeps on talking. She doesn't answer.

"You must save my son! You must save my grandchildren!" she says.

"Who is your son?"

"He is here."

"Who? Your son?"

She nods. "And so is Father!"

"Oh," I say. I back up a few more steps. "Why don't you go back where you came from? I can't help you. Stop bothering me, okay? Can you do that for me?"

"Only the pure of heart will survive his wrath!" she screams, startling the hell out of me. I almost drop the Maglite.

And then she's gone. *Poof!* I hate it when ghosts do that. It's very annoying.

I'm breathing hard. My heart is racing. I'm sweating in spite of the cool breeze. *This shit's gotta stop!*

I quickly go back inside. *Just forget about it, man!* I tell myself, but I can't. Walking my rounds now is creeping me out. I feel as if something bad is about to happen. I vividly recall finding Peter's head on the shelf. I consider running back outside, getting in my car, and driving away, but I don't actually go for it. Like a good little security guard, I do my duty for a lousy thirteen bucks an hour. I keep checking things out. I'm suddenly worried about Sue. I don't like her being alone in her office. I cruise over to make sure she's okay.

The two men with guns intrigue Sabbah as he follows them in the form of a fly. They're about midway through the warehouse, not far from where poor Peter lost his empty little head. Sabbah buzzes by the left ear of one of the big men, causing him to slap and swat.

"Damn fly!" Big Dude says.

"I hate flies," Other Big Dude says. "They carry all kinds of germs, you know that?"

"Yeah, I do. Gross little suckers. Wonder why God ever made them in the first place."

Sabbah laughs as he lands on the other man's head, right on the bald spot on top.

"Damn! There it is again!" Other Big Dude says. He swipes at Sabbah, but Sabbah easily flies out of the way.

"Aggressive little shit, isn't he?" Big Dude says.

It's time to rock 'n roll! Sabbah says, feeling a surge of joy unlike any other he's experienced as a demon. *It's time!* Chanting quietly, he summons the dark one's power, and instantly he begins to transform. His body expands. His wings drop off. He suddenly becomes himself again. A swirling black mist surrounds him as he watches the two men continue walking down the long, dimly lit aisle in the middle of the warehouse.

"Gentlemen," Sabbah says.

"What? You say something?" Big Dude asks.

"No."

"Well, I just heard something. A voice. A weird-sounding voice."

"I didn't hear anything," Other Big Dude says.

"Gentlemen! Turn around and face your fate!" Sabbah cries.

Both men spin around. Sabbah takes great delight in their shocked expressions, the fear that obviously grips both men.

"What the hell?" Big Dude says, drawing his gun.

Other Big Dude draws his weapon and shouts, "RCMP! Freeze!"

14

KIND SPIRITS

The present, outside Montreal, Brouchard Inc., Thursday, 11:03 to 11:30 p.m.

When I get to Sue's office, I'm surprised to find Jean Claude sitting in one of the chairs in front of her desk. Sue looks upset.

"Howdy," I say.

They both turn to look at me as I stand in the doorway.

"Oh, hi, Michael," Sue says.

"Michael," Jean Claude says.

"Just making my rounds and figured I'd drop by," I say. "Mr. Brouchard still here?"

"Yeah, he is," Jean Claude says. "Kind of strange, since his kids are sick. I figured he'd have gone straight home after the meeting."

I stroll in and sit down beside Jean Claude. I shoot Sue a smile. "I'm not interrupting anything personal, am I?"

They both look uncomfortable, so I know I actually have stuck my nose into something. I just don't know what.

"Uh, no, not really," Sue says. "Jean Claude and I are just making contingency plans in case some of our people quit."

"Yeah, that's right," Jean Claude says.

"You gotta figure on losing some personnel," I say. "That would only be natural, even if Brouchard has something on 'em."

"What do you mean by that?" Jean Claude asks, his voice defensive. His posture stiffens, and so does Sue's.

"Hit a nerve, eh?"

They both remain silent.

"You guys are something else, man! I've been doing some digging. It seems like most, if not all, of your employees have secrets. Or rap sheets. Stuff that makes them tough to hire under normal circumstances."

"You'd be wise to mind your own business, Michael," Jean Claude says. "You might get hurt if you don't."

I laugh. "You mean like Mannie and Peter?"

"Well, you never—"

Sue's scream cuts Jean Claude off as she leaps up from her chair and points to the open door behind Jean Claude and me. We both spin around, and Jean Claude's jaw drops.

"Wha-what—?" Jean Claude tries to speak, but he can't finish his sentence. He just stares all bug-eyed at the vaporous forms of two men standing in the doorway.

I can't believe what I'm seeing either, though I know I'm less surprised than Jean Claude and Sue. I've been seeing a lot of strange crap lately. I'm getting used to it.

"Good evening, ladies and germs!" says Mannie's ghost.

He's fading in and out, which is cool with me, because he looks really, really disgusting. He's completely nude. All his skin is black and peeling off. Other gray pieces just hang limply in big irregularly shaped sheets, like plastic wrap or something. Half his face looks like a lion has munched out on it, and one of his arms is missing. Oozy gross clumps of dried up pus or plasma speckle his contorted body. Peter stands next to him in his bloody uniform. His head is back in place, but you can see big staples and sutures holding it on. He looks like a terrible imitation of Frankenstein's monster, only much more scary and ugly. All he's missing are the neck bolts.

"How is everything going tonight?" Mannie asks.

"*Oh . . . my . . . Lord!*" Sue screams.

The sound of her dropping in a faint makes Jean Claude and me momentarily turn away from the ghosts. I rush to Sue, who's sprawled out on the floor behind her desk with her mouth wide open. I lift her into my arms.

"Aw, how nice," Peter says. "Big M's gonna protect cute little Susie Q!"

Jean Claude moves toward the ghosts. "Get out of here! Leave us! I rebuke you!"

Both ghosts laugh hysterically. They're laughing so hard they double over and hold their stomachs.

"You see what a tough guy he is?" Mannie asks Peter.

"Yeah, real tough! Like, sure! As tough as a cream puff!" Peter says. Peter jumps forward, stops one inch from Jean Claude's nose, and shouts, "Boo!"

Jean Claude makes a gurgling noise and faints. I prop Sue up against the wall in a sitting position and stand up, facing the ghosts.

"Now look what you did!" Mannie says.

"Dudes, man!" I say. "Don't fuck with us, okay! You'll give me a damn coronary! What's up with you guys, anyway? What are you doing here?"

Both ghosts laugh. They close the door and take the two seats in front of Sue's desk. I remain standing. I don't feel much like sitting anyway.

"We're actually here to warn you, man!" Peter says.

"Yeah. Like, uh, warn you, dude!" Mannie says. Mannie crosses his legs.

I look away. I don't want to see his burnt junk, but it's too late. *Delete image!*

"What's the matter?" Mannie asks.

Peter spins his head around three hundred sixty degrees.

"Aw, man! Don't do that, dude!" I say to Peter. "That's just too fuckin' gross, man!"

Both ghosts think that's hilarious.

"Do it again!" Mannie shouts.

"Warn me about what?" I ask, trying to get them back on track.

Sue groans. I look over at her as she comes to and sees her unearthly guests. She makes a whimpering noise a little like a puppy having a bad hair day. Her eyes go wide, and she passes out again.

"She's having a real bad night," Peter says. "Serve's the bitch right."

"Yeah, serves the bitch right!" Mannie says.

"I thought Sue gave you both a break," I say, becoming interested in their hostility toward her, though I know the HR department in any company is the most hated.

"She did," Peter says. "She gives us all a break, and then she makes us slaves to fuckin' Brouchard, the preacher from the gates of hell!"

"Yeah, it's like that, Michael. The gates of hell!"

Peter spins his head again for effect.

"I told you not to do that!" I shout. "Come on, Peter! Cut it out!"

"Sorry," Peter says.

Jean Claude opens his eyes. Both ghosts get up from their chairs, walk a few steps, and lean over Jean Claude real close. They both scream, "*Booga, booga, booga! Boo!*"

Sputtering and stuttering and gurgling, Jean Claude struggles to his feet and runs out of Sue's office. We can all hear his raised voice fading as he races away, like the Doppler effect when an ambulance or a whistling train goes by and the sound changes, growing fainter by the second and slightly distorted. It's exactly like that, and it strikes me as hilarious. Now the three of us are cracking up, hooting and hollering and having a hell of a time. Sue wakes up again. She sees us.

"*Oh . . . my . . . Lord!*" Sue screams again. "*Oh Lordie!* Ma-Man-Mannie, is that you? Pah-Pah-Peetah? *Oh . . . my . . . God!*" Sue struggles to stand, but she blacks out again, slumping back against the wall. Her head lolls off to the left. Her blonde curls cover part of her pretty face. She looks as if she's sleeping, and I suppose she is, in a way.

"I'm tellin' ya!" Peter says to Mannie. "That chick's gonna need a shrink after all this crap!"

After we all stop laughing again, I say, "So what do you want to warn me about?" I'm now genuinely curious. I think I have a good idea of what's going down, but confirmation from two ghosts would be peachy. I'm grateful that I've seen the devil creature and the sexy ghost in white robes. It's been sort of like prep school for the big-time weird I sense is coming.

"The dark one is here," both ghosts say at once. They've suddenly gone serious.

"You mean the one who killed you guys?"

"He's small potatoes," Peter says.

"Dude, man, he's gnarly, but he's not the one you have to worry about most!" Mannie says.

"Yeah, the other one is a real badass. He's here, man, and you better—"

"The other one? What other one?" I ask.

Gunshots ring out. *Boom! Boom! Boom!*

Sabbah grins as the bullets pass right through him and ricochet off the concrete walls and racks of metal parts in the warehouse. He laughs at the two frightened men, and he swoops down on them.

"Run! Run!" Big Dude shouts.

Both men turn to run down the central aisle of the warehouse, but Sabbah swirls past them, blocking their path. They turn and run the other way, and Sabbah does the same thing, blocking them again. Tall racks hem them in on either side.

"You cannot escape!" Sabbah cries, his face twisted in a hideous grin. "You are mine! You all are mine!"

Sabbah raises his arms and points at the men. He begins chanting louder and louder. The men are frozen in place as streams of black vapor shoot from Sabbah's fingertips. In moments, the vapor surrounds the men.

"I can't move! I can't—" Other Big Dude screams.

"Me either!"

Manipulating his hands, Sabbah focuses on the guns. The men raise their gun hands, their terror obvious as they watch themselves moving involuntarily, as if they are puppets.

"Yes! That's it, my little friends," Sabbah roars. He continues chanting.

"No, no! Don't do it!" Big Dude screams as his companion brings his gun up and aims it at Big Dude's chest. "For the love of God, don't—"

Other Big Dude fires. He's clearly horrified at what he's done, and Sabbah laughs. He continues chanting.

"Now you! Now you, my little friend!" Sabbah shouts.

Other Big Dude puts the gun to his temple and pulls the trigger. The bullet explodes his skull in a cloud of red mist and gray brain matter. Gore creates a beautiful mosaic of bone, brain, and thick red blood on a large cardboard box on a shelf as the man drops to the gray concrete floor at Sabbah's feet.

"Ah, the end is near now!" Sabbah says, his voice calm. "The end is so very near I can taste it!" A snake emerges from his robes and curls around his right arm. Sabbah brings the snake close to his face. The snake's forked tongue darts out, licking Sabbah's old wrinkled cheek. "Hello, old friend," Sabbah says. "Are you ready for some real fun?"

The gunshots freak me out. I guess they also scare the ghosts, who both scream and disappear. Sue opens her eyes.

"Are they gone?" she asks, her eyes wide, her hands clasped against her ample breasts.

"I think so!" I say. I'm trying to control my breathing and my heart rate. I wasn't kidding about having a coronary. I'm young and in good shape, but the crap that's been going on is enough to crank anybody's thumper.

"What's happening?" Sue asks, and then she breaks down in tears.

"I don't know," I say, kneeling in front of her. I take her hands in mine. "I just heard gunshots. We got to get you and the rest of the people out of here."

"Gunshots? From the officers?"

"I don't know who else it could be," I say. I stand, pulling her to her feet. "Come on! Let's get the hell outta here!"

15

THE HUNTED

The present, outside Montreal, Brouchard Inc., Thursday, 11:32 to 12:24 p.m.

As Sue and I leave her office and head toward the empty admin section, she stops short and grabs my arm. She looks scared. Really scared.

"We've got to get Paul! Paul's in his office!"

"Unless the dude's deaf, he heard the gunfire," I say.

"We have to check on him!"

I relent, and we both run to his office. I pound on his door.

"Mr. Brouchard? You in there?"

Nothing.

"Anybody home?" I yell.

Still nothing.

"Paul! Paul! Open up, please!" Sue pounds on the door too.

"Fine," I say, wondering why the guy hasn't rushed out of his office already. I try the door, and find it's unlocked. We burst in and see the office is empty. The boss's briefcase is open on his desk. I go over to the desk and pick up a mug sitting near the phone.

"Coffee's still warm," I say. "Maybe he got out before we did."

"That's impossible!" Sue says. "He'd have had to go right by us!"

"Well, whatever," I say. "We got to get the people out. Brouchard can go to hell for all I care!"

"Michael!"

I take Sue's arm and drag her out of Brouchard's office. "We don't have time to fuck around, Sue! We got some serious shit going down right now!"

We round a corner and see that the halls are filled with frightened people. Jean Claude is shouting for everyone to run for the exits. Keeping Sue close to me, I join Jean Claude in herding the employees toward the fire doors. The first wave reaches the nearest door, and one of the workers pushes the steel lever down to get out.

"Oh my God! The door won't open!" shouts a cute brunette wearing a greasy smock. "We're trapped! Oh my God, we're trapped!"

I push through the crowd and try the door. It's definitely locked or jammed. "Jean Claude! Try the next one!" I shout.

"No good!" he screams over the increasing din.

Whoa, this ain't good! I think. "Everyone to the lobby!" I shout. I keep Sue close. I don't want her to get separated from me as Jean Claude and I act like traffic cops. We try to keep the herd from stampeding and only just manage. "Everything'll be cool! Just don't run! Don't panic!" I yell.

"Jean Claude, can you do a head count?" Sue struggles to be heard over the noise. "I think we're missing some people!"

He says he's trying, but it's hard for him to tell in all the confusion.

We move as a massive wave of humanity down the hall and into the expansive lobby. I push through the screaming men and women and try the door. It's locked too! I try my master key. It doesn't work. The panic quotient rises exponentially. Everyone is scared shitless that a gunman will appear at any moment and open fire on the crowd, and they're smart to be scared. I know a gunman could appear at any moment. Those officers were shooting at something—and then it hits me! They could be shooting at the devil creature!

I ask myself, *Which would be worse? A crazed killer with a gun? Or a crazed tail-beating, teeth-gnashing, ugly-ass devil creature ready for a midnight snack?*

Thinking fast, I grab the receptionist's chair and throw it through the glass window with Brouchard Inc. stenciled on it. The glass shatters and the burglar alarm goes off. It's really loud, and people put their hands over the ears. Jean Claude heaves another chair through what's left of the window, and more glass shatters. Jean Claude and I smash the glass shards around the edge of the window so that escaping employees don't be cut to ribbons.

"Everybody out! One at a time!" I say, and I start directing traffic again. "Everyone get in a line!"

A big guy pushes a middle-aged assembly worker out of the way. I get in his face big time. "You want me to ram your head down into your ass, you do that again!" I'm exactly his height, and he's got about twenty pounds on me, but he's out of shape and he's about ten years older. He's no match for me, and he knows it.

"Sorry, Michael," he says and steps back.

Sue and I help the lady up and over the bottom of the window.

"You go next, Sue," I say.

She shakes her head. "Not until we know we've gotten everyone out."

Just then the lights dim. Dozens of people scream, both men and women, as the fire alarm goes off, adding its shrieks and whoops to the burglar alarm.

"Oh fuck! Can this get any better?" I say to no one in particular. "Everybody stay calm! Stay calm! There's no need to panic!"

It seems to take forever, but we get the last of the people in the lobby out the front window.

"Okay, Sue, you're next!" I say.

Again she says she's not going. "I did a head count. We're missing Tina, Chandi, Pierre, Adrian, Jacques, Francois, and Martin. They're in the far wing."

"Yeah, I know where they are," I say. "Assembly Room 21."

"I'll go check on them," Jean Claude says.

I can see people outside running to their cars and burning rubber out of the parking lot, a very sensible course of action under the circumstances. The alarms keep squealing like stuck pigs. The emergency lights go on, but it's still pretty dark.

"You call 911, Jean Claude? Sue?"

They both say they did.

"To report shots fired or a fire?" I ask.

"I think 911 is going to have a meltdown with so many calls coming in," Jean Claude says. "From all the people outside, I mean."

"Good point. Hey, you smell that?" I ask.

A whiff of acrid smoke comes through the air-conditioning ducts, indicating that the fire is real.

"Where are those two policemen?" Sue asks, barely controlling her emotions. "What were they shooting at?"

I look at Jean Claude, and he looks at me. I've been wondering the same thing ever since this whole shebang got started. I'm worried. Very worried. If those guys aren't on the scene, then that can only mean they can't get on the scene, for some reason. I'm trying not to picture the reason, which I think most likely is a big, hairy devil creature on the loose.

"I don't know, Sue," I lie.

"This can't be good," Jean Claude says.

"I know," I say.

We all stand there for a few seconds, numb from the shock and fear.

"Can you shut that alarm off?" I ask Jean Claude. "It's driving me batshit!"

He actually laughs and slaps me on the back. "Me too, dude!" he says, mimicking me.

I see he's smiling, so I don't get pissed off at him. "Well, *dude*, can you turn the sound off, at least?"

"Yeah," he says, "we can kill the sound from the main control panel on our way to Assembly Room 21. We got people trapped in here, and we got to get 'em out!"

"Roger that," I say.

Jean Claude gives me a confused look. "You were in the military?" he asks as I take Sue by the hand and we all run deeper into the factory. The smoke gets progressively thicker.

"Hell, no! I just watch a lot of old war movies!"

"Oh," he replies.

We get to the control panel. I whip out my Maglite because, strangely, the emergency lights are all out in this section. I shine the Mag on the panel while Jean Claude disables the sound on the alarms. All goes silent. Spooky silent. "The station will still get the alert," he says.

"Yeah, kinda figured that," I say.

"It's gonna take a while for any help to get here," Sue says. "We're pretty far out."

"Yeah, kinda figured that too," I say.

"We're on our own," Jean Claude says.

"Yeah, kinda figured that," I say.

"Will you shut the fuck up?" Jean Claude says.

"Yeah, kinda—"

"Let's go!" Sue says, her voice calm and authoritative.

Jean Claude and I comply. The three of us turn and run down a hall leading to the warehouse, which we have to cross before we can get to Assembly Room 21. As we enter the warehouse, lit in dim red and white lights, a cloud of smoke reaches us. I swear I see a tail disappear around one of the racks just as we move forward. I hear the familiar *click-click-click*ing, the big-dog-nails-on-tile sound I'd heard in Brouchard's office, and I know we're not alone. I stop and shine my light along a nearby rack.

"Why are you stopping?" Jean Claude asks.

I don't answer. I keep rifling through the stuff on the nearby racks. Jean Claude and Sue come back to join me. We're all near the entrance of the warehouse. At last I find what I'm looking for, a long, slender length of pipe. I pick it up, hefting it in my hand. Jean Claude smiles.

"Dude, great minds think alike!" he says as he picks up another length of pipe. "I was thinking the same damn thing."

"What?" Sue asks, totally clueless.

"Head whacker," Jean Claude says. "Or door opener."

Or devil-creature banger, I think, but I don't say it. Don't want to get into the devil-creature crap. I figure the thing will make itself known any minute now anyway.

"Come on!" I say, and I lead the way with my Maglite. I'm more on edge than ever. The smoke is getting thicker, and I swear I can hear pounding on a door in the distance. What I'm more worried about is the clicking sound I hear behind us. I tense, ready to defend Sue and Jean Claude if that thing attacks.

"You hear that?" Sue whispers. "Stop! Listen!"

We all stop.

"Sounds like someone's beating on a door," Jean Claude whispers. "Hey, that's got to be our people!"

"Shh!" Sue says, putting her right index finger up to her luscious lips. "Lord, I swear I heard something. Like a big ol' hound dog."

"You got any hounds in here?" I ask.

"Of course not," she says.

"Then it's something else," I say.

We strain our ears, but we can't hear anything. Everything is silent in the smoky shadows, except for the distant banging. We continue on our way, and about two minutes later we find the dead officers in Lake Superior pools of blood and gore. The blood looks black in the eerie low light.

"Ahh!" Sue screams and promptly faints.

I catch her just in time to keep her from smashing her head open on the concrete floor.

"Son of a bitch," Jean Claude says.

"You can say that again," I say, standing up from making Sue comfortable for her faint.

"Son of a bitch," Jean Claude repeats.

I don't laugh. I put the pipe down and pick up one of the pistols, wiping the blood off on Big Dude's ruined suit. I check that the safety is on, and I pull back the slide to make sure there's a round in the chamber. Then I pop the magazine to see how full it is. Jean Claude watches me, his jaw set, his eyes steely.

"You sure you weren't in the military, Michael?" he asks, stooping to pick up the other officer's gun.

"Sure as shit," I say.

We stare at the bodies, sizing up the scene.

"You seeing what I'm seeing?" I ask.

Jean Claude nods. "Two bodies. Two guns. Looks like that guy blew his own brains out," Jean Claude says, pointing at Other Big Dude.

"Exactly," I say, "which is way too hinky, man. It's like something made them turn their guns on themselves."

Jean Claude nods. Sue groans, opens her eyes, and finds herself looking face-to-face into half-headed Other Big Dude. She screams again. "Oh, Lord bless my soul! God protect me! God protect us!"

Sue gets to her feet, but she's looking pretty wobbly, which I guess is natural.

I hear the clicking noise again, and this time I see a black shadow appear right behind us. It's silhouetted against a dim background of red and white near a fire exit. I distinctly see two horns, long spindly legs, and a tail moving back and forth across the floor. The tail makes a swishing sound I know the others can hear.

"There's someone in here!" Sue whispers.

Jean Claude steps close to her, gun ready.

"Or some*thing*," I say.

"What the hell are you talking about?" Jean Claude asks.

"You'll see!"

All of a sudden the dark form leaps straight up in the air and lands on a tall rack. Jean Claude opens up on it. Bullets twang and ping as they ricochet. Then the form is gone. All is quiet, except for the ringing in my ears. I look over at Sue. She's got her left and right index fingers poked into her ears.

"You missed," I say to Jean Claude.

"What?" he asks.

"I said you missed it!"

"Ah, oh—yeah. Guess so! What the hell was that thing?"

"Oh Lord! It looked like the devil!" Sue says.

"Whatever it is, it's probably really pissed," I say. "Let's book!"

Another cloud of acrid smoke drifts down the aisle toward us.

"We got to go! Now!" I yell.

I take Sue by the hand, and we all rush toward the exit of the warehouse. That devil creature is a shifty little son of a bitch. It could be hiding anywhere, and I figure that it's probably pretty pissed about being shot at. The last thing I want to tangle with is a pissed-off devil creature, but it looks to me as if that's definitely in the cards. We burst out of the warehouse on the other side. I stop and lock the steel door behind us, which I know in my heart of hearts is going to do about as much good as trying to get toothpaste back in the tube. Now we can clearly hear pounding and screaming coming from down the hall, and the sound sends chills through me even though I'm sweating my balls off.

"Come on!" I shout. "Looks like the fire's in there! With our missing people!"

I'm on the run with my two companions, semiautomatic in hand, a round in the chamber. That's when the laughing starts. At first I think I'm hearing things, and I dismiss it. My heart is beating in my ears, which are still ringing from Jean Claude's *Dirty Harry* routine. Then I hear it again, demonic and otherworldly.

Ha, ha, hee, hee, ho, ho, hee, ha! Snort! Snort! Snuffle, ah!

We all freeze in our tracks.

"It's in front of us!" Sue says. "How'd it get in front of us? We just left whatever that thing was in the warehouse!"

16

THE RECKONING

The present, outside Montreal, Brouchard Inc., Thursday, 12:25 to 12:56 p.m.

I peer ahead of us into the shadows and wafts of smoke, and I can just make out the devil creature. It's slowly walking toward us. We advance toward the door of Assembly Room 21, keeping an eye on the monster.

"I'll distract it while you guys free our people!" Jean Claude says.

I say okay as we all get to the door. Jean Claude keeps going. The devil creature is laughing its ass off now. I glance in its direction, and I'm shocked to see that it has two little friends. They look identical to Big Daddy, except they're only as big as little kids.

"Oh my!" Sue says.

Jean Claude screams and rushes the creatures, his pipe in one hand and the gun in the other.

I pound on the door and tell everyone inside to stand back. I push Sue out of the way and fire a couple rounds into the lock. Sparks fly. The bullets dig small craters in the concrete wall across from the door. With all my strength, I kick the door. It gives way just as I hear Jean Claude scream in agony.

"Oh Lord, they've got him! They're killing Jean Claude!" Sue screams.

She's right. Jean Claude is sprawled on his back. He's fighting the two little devil creatures that are standing on his chest and sticking him with little pitchforks. Blood fountains from the holes, and I know Jean Claude's heart is pumping its last pumps. I feel bad about that. Turns out he wasn't such a prick after all. Big Daddy Devil laughs as he watches. For the first time, I hear the big devil creature speak, and it sounds a little like Paul Brouchard.

"Yes, my children! Finish him! Kill him! You will dine on his flesh for a healthy, hearty breakfast!"

I don't have time to think. Instead, Sue and I rush into Assembly Room 21. Jacques is the first one to reach the door.

"Thank God you got here in time!" he says.

Tina and Chandi are right on Jacques's heels. When they see Sue, Chandi, who's smacking a big wad of bubblegum, says, "I quit!"

"Yeah, me too!" Tina says. "This place really sucks! People shooting guns or something, and . . . uh . . . like mysterious fires that could blow our asses off aren't part of our job descriptions! Right, Chandi?"

Chandi blows a big pink bubble with her gum. It pops. "Yeah! We both quit!"

Sue rolls her eyes at the girls as Martin, Pierre, and Adrian bring up the rear with Francois.

"The fire is getting pretty bad," Pierre says. "It just started all by itself near the welding department. We heard the alarm and tried to get out, but all the doors locked on us! We also thought we heard gunshots just before the shit hit the fan!"

"Yeah, like we said!" Tina says. "We quit! You can take your job and shove it up your tight little ass!"

"Holy shit!" Chandi yells. "Look! Watch out behind you!"

"What the hell are those things?" Tina yells. *"Eek! Ah! Oh my God!"*

Sue and I turn around. The devil creatures run toward us, their pitchforks lowered like spears. They've got us cornered. I rush toward them, firing as I go, but the bullets seem to pass right through them. Jacques picks up a spanner and charges along with me, but the little shits are quick. They drive us back. Francois joins in the battle, but it does no good. Every time we think we've hit a devil creature, it vanishes. It's as if the creatures aren't real, and yet they're doing serious damage. Have done serious damage.

"The big one looks like Mr. Brouchard!" squeals Chandi, spitting her gum out and backing up. "Oh my God! It's the boss!"

As Jacques and I confront the creatures, I can see some weird resemblance to Brouchard, but I chock it up to the panic of the moment. Besides, I'm about to get my ass handed to me by the two little-shit devil creatures that are rushing in to stab me in the thighs, or worse, somewhere a little higher.

"Look out, Michael!" Adrian yells.

"I see 'em," I say. "Martin, Adrian, Pierre! Get the fire extinguisher from the hall and put that fire out! If those acetylene tanks go they'll take us all out!"

I take a few more swipes at the little creatures, jumping back before they can get me. "Go! Go! Go!" I yell to the men.

They hesitate, but then they rush past the devil creatures. For a moment, it occurs to me that they might just run away.

Suddenly, everything stops cold. The devil creatures freeze. They're looking past me at something in the back of the room. I don't dare turn my back on them. I'm just glad there's a lull that'll give the guys time to get the fire extinguisher. Then I hear more laughter, a low sinister laugh that makes the hairs on my neck stand up straight. Sue, Chandi, and Tina scream. Sue drops to the floor in a dead faint.

"Michael," Jacques says, "you're not gonna believe this!"

"Try me."

"There . . . there's some weird demon thing behind us."

"Well, there are three weird demon things in front of us."

"I'm not kidding!" Jacques says.

"You are all doomed! You are the guilty ones! Your souls are damned to the fires of hell for your sins! My children will feast upon your flesh and feed the rest to the hounds of hell!" the voice booms.

"Just what I need," I say to Jacques. "Demons to the right of us. Demons to the left of us, demons—"

I whirl around for just a sec and see an old man floating in the air. A cloud of black mist surrounds him. A nasty-looking snake is wrapped around his right arm. The weird thing is that the guy's wearing an eye patch, kinda like a pirate from hell or something. He almost looks funny, but not quite.

I hear Martin, Pierre, and Adrian rush into the room with the fire extinguisher.

"What the fuck?" Pierre says.

"Oh no, not another one!" Martin says.

Adrian remains silent. Francois crosses himself.

"This place is totally, like, fucked up," Chandi says.

"Silence!" Sabbah commands.

I whirl around again to keep an eye on the devil creatures, and I'm stunned to see them scamper past me and kneel in front of the dude with the eye patch.

Sue comes to, sees Eye Patch, and promptly passes out again. I suspect she's going to have one hell of a headache, if she doesn't end up as devil's food.

"Run! Get to that fire before the tanks blow!" I scream. "We don't have a moment to lose!"

The three guys hesitate. They're frozen in place out of astonishment and fear.

"Go! Go! Go! Pay no attention to the dude behind the eye patch!" I yell.

Only Martin moves. He rushes past the group, with the fire extinguisher, and begins spraying the base of the fire. The flames are dangerously close to the acetylene tanks now. They could go at any second. The idea of that scares me as much as these funky creatures. Suddenly, I see the sexy ghost in the white robes. She materializes right in front of Eye Patch and the devils. I'm starting to wonder what other creatures or ghosts will show up. Mannie and Peter perhaps? I think this is one party they'd rather miss.

"You must stop this!" sexy ghost says. "Father, you have done enough!"

"It is you who are to blame!" Eye Patch says, pointing an accusatory finger at her. The snake uncoils a little and hisses. The devil creatures stare at both figures, and then they get off their knees.

"That's it!" Tina yells, "we're outta here! Come on, Chandi! Run!"

Chandi and Tina run for the door, and in an instant the devil creatures rush past me. I take a swipe at one on the way by, but it does no good. All three devil creatures jump the girls. Big Daddy rips Chandi's arm off. His two little friends perforate Tina before any of us can do a thing. The blood is Lake Superior again, and I'm getting sick and tired of seeing it. That kinda stuff gets old real fast, and yet I'm unsure of what to do. Nothing seems able to stop the creatures, or whatever the hell they are. I can see the lady in white is royally pissed now. She rears up and slaps the devil creatures, and they back away from her.

"You have done enough!" she screams at Big Daddy. Big Daddy cowers.

"No, it is you who have done enough!" Eye Patch says to the lady in white. "You are as much behind their creation as I am! We share in the blood!"

A tremendous explosion rips through the room. I'm rocketed off my feet, and I come down hard. I hear men screaming. I look for Sue, but I don't see her. I don't hear her shouting, "Oh Lord," in her Southern twang, so I imagine she's still out cold. The heat from the acetylene tanks is intense. I look toward the door and see one of the guys, Pierre, I think, looking like a Roman candle as he drops in the hallway. He thrashes for a few seconds, and then he goes still.

Another deadster, I think. Body count's gonna be high!

"Help! Help me!"

I recognize Sue's voice. It sounds weak. I hear lots of coughing. Clearly not everyone is dead. Martin has to be, since he was trying to put the fire out and was right next to the tanks. Roman candle Pierre is. Poked and perforated Jean Claude is. The others? I can't be sure. I stay low to the floor where the good air is and move toward the sound of Sue's voice. Through the smoke and fire I can see Eye Patch, the lady in white, and the three devil creatures. They're standing in a group, which strikes me as pretty weird.

"You're killing the innocent!" the sexy ghost lady says to Eye Patch.

"Innocent? Hardly," Sabbah says. "The dark one delights in feasting on the souls of the innocent. Those are the most valuable of all, but there are so few of them. So, so few! The souls of the guilty must suffice, and we have plenty of them right here! Plenty of murderers. Mannie, Jean Claude, Peter, and Martin! All murderers! And these apparently innocent young women are guilty too! Tina helped Chandi kill her roommate's pregnant girlfriend just so Chandi could have the boyfriend all to herself! Can you imagine that?"

Eye Patch lets out a laugh that practically deafens me. I see a form ahead in the smoke. It's Sue! I recognize her sexy legs. I crawl toward her, coughing my lungs out.

"But why are my grandchildren cursed?" the lady ghost cries. "It was I who failed you. My son did not fail you. It was me!"

"Your son is part of you! So he failed me as much as you did. His children are part of you too! The guilty must be punished! Bad things happen, and sometimes bad things happen to the innocent, like to my beautiful Suri! Like to those two policemen! But the deaths must come!"

The sexy ghost lady puts both hands over her face and begins to cry. It's as if she's given up the fight, and I think maybe she has.

"Peter robbed and raped old ladies!" Sabbah screams. "He did it for years! He only went away for armed robbery, but I know what he really did. How guilty he was! And then there is Francois! He brought his teenage girlfriend to have an abortion, an abortion at the hands of none other than Paul Henri Brouchard, the supposedly unblemished priest! She died a terrible death! An innocent if there ever was one! And Adrian! He is as corrupt as the worst. His heart is rotten! His soul will soon belong to the dark one!"

I'm listening to Eye Patch's tirade, and even in all the confusion I'm putting it all together. The mention of Paul Henri Brouchard clicks. The clips! All the clips must have been news stories about the crimes of the guilty on Brouchard's list! Even Brouchard's adoptive father was among the guilty! Through the billowing smoke I can see the clawed flipper feet and spindly legs of the devil creatures with their long tails dragging behind. The devil creatures have moved off from the demon and the ghost. *Oh shit! They're looking for survivors!* I hurry up and get to Sue as I hear stabbing squishing noises very near to me on the left, and I know it's probably another Brouchard employee biting the dust.

"Oh no! No! Ahh!"

Yep, that was Adrian. Go! Get a move on, dude, if you don't want to end up as a French fry!

I hear Francois start screaming. "No, don't let them kill me! Michael! Anybody! Somebody help me!" Francois shouts.

I can see him through the smoke and fire. The devil creatures are all on him, stabbing him with pitchforks and ripping his face off! It's really gross. Eye Patch is laughing again.

"Sue! Sue!" I say as I crawl next to her. "Wake up, Sue!"

She moans and coughs. "Wha-who?"

"It's me! Michael! Come on, we gotta get out of here before more of the tanks blow! Or before we're devil dinners!"

Taking a chance, I struggle to my feet, dragging Sue up with me. She sags, doubles over with coughing.

"I can't make it," she says between coughs.

"You have to!"

Francois stops howling.

Still another deadster!

"You've got to make it!" I sweep Sue up in my arms and make a run for it.

"Go!" Sabbah laughs. "Go, my children! There are more delicious snacks for you!"

"Stop!" the ghost lady shouts.

I'm out the door and moving as fast as I can down the hall. Sue is unconscious again. No surprise there. Another explosion blasts behind me, knocking me down. In seconds, the devil creatures are on me. I stand up, hefting my pipe, but they ignore me and go for Sue! I'm swiping at them, but I can't get them off her. Jacques appears at my side, and we both fight the devil creature. Eye Patch walks out of a wall of fire.

"There's nothing we can do for her!" Jacques yells. "She's dead! If we don't haul ass, we're going to be dead too!"

I can see he's right, and I feel badly for her. Was she one of the innocents that bad things happen to? Did she have a story like the rest of them? Did Jacques? We don't have time to mess around. As we turn to run, I catch a glimpse of Big Daddy ripping Sue's head off and taking a big bite.

"Man, this place is too messed up!" I yell.

"You got that right!" Jacques replies.

We race through the warehouse. Sirens wail over the noise of the fire. Suddenly, we see firemen rush toward us!

"Oh, thank Yahweh!" I say, and I really mean it.

Epilogue

The present, Montreal,
Laurent Barra's office, Friday afternoon

I'm sitting across from my boss, my face bandaged and my hair partly burned off. I even lost one of my eyebrows, so I look pretty ridiculous. I've got burns on my arms and legs too. I'm frankly a mess, but I've been worse. I'm just glad my time at Brouchard Inc. is over. Too much has happened for me to ever go back there when Brouchard rebuilds. And he will. He's said as much to the newspapers. Men like him, evil men, almost always seem to come out on top. It's the little guys like me who always get screwed.

"So they all died," Laurent says. It's a statement, not a question.

"Every last one of them, except Jacques."

I've kept back some things from my boss, like the ghosts, demons, and devil creatures. Nobody would believe me, with the possible exception of Jacques, and like me, he's not talking either. Sometimes it's best to just keep quiet.

"You think Brouchard was mixed up in this? You think he set the fire for the insurance money?"

"I'd bet on it, but we can't prove jack," I say. "It's just a shame. All those people. They were guilty of crap in their lives—but who isn't? They got burned up just because a rich dude wants to cash an insurance check. It's just not right."

I sigh, shake my head, and lean back in my chair.

"Well, I'm glad you got out safe. You and that Jacques guy. Papers say you're a hero, you know, what with helping all the rest of the people get out before the explosion," Laurent says. He hesitates and gives me a long, hard look. "You're not telling me everything, Michael. I can tell."

I look back at him and say he's wrong.

"My contacts at the police say the death of the two cops is being ruled a homicide, even though ballistics show the rounds came from their own guns. They're saying the killer or killers ambushed them before setting the place on fire. They say they're looking into Brouchard's past to see who might have it in for him, and yet you're saying it was Brouchard himself who set all this in motion. I don't get it. I'm missing something."

I assure him that there was no killer other than Brouchard.

"But you can't prove it," Laurent says.

"Like I said."

Laurent picks up a pen, taps his desk with it, and then puts it down. "Well, I'm going to have some people keep an eye on this guy. If he's dirty, he'll make a mistake at some point, and we can take him down when he does."

"That would be nice," I say. "Are we done for now? I'm bushed."

Laurent smiles. "Just one more thing. You give any more thought to getting your PI license?"

I stand up and offer my boss my hand. We shake. "Let me get some R & R first, Laurent. I gotta sort things out in my head."

"Sure, Michael. Sure."

I say goodbye to Laurent and then turn and walk out of his office. The summer sun is shining brightly. The sky is blue. The air doesn't have one bit of humidity in it. Overall, it's a pretty nice day to be alive. A pretty nice day—except that my name is on Brouchard's list, and I think I know why.